For my parents

I0521340

SIX
DEAD
SPOTS

SIX DEAD SPOTS

GREGOR XANE

new dollar pulp

ohio

SIX DEAD SPOTS

A New Dollar Pulp Book

Published by New Dollar Pulp

Cover Art & Design By:

N the **NERDGENCY**

thenerdgency.com

Acknowledgements

I'd like to thank everyone who so graciously took the time to look at this thing in its many earlier versions. Thank you for your helpful feedback Worm, Creekbird, Ruben, Big Brown, and Mr. Jason Parent. I'd also like to thank John Overwine for services rendered and Bruce Bethke for the recent confidence boost.

Most of all, I'd like to thank my extremely tolerant family. It's impossible to imagine a wife and two daughters more brilliant and lovely.

SIX
DEAD
SPOTS

Chapter 1

Frank woke up and found five dead spots on his body. He discovered them in the shower. He found the first one while lathering his chest. A circle of skin, the size of a large collector's coin, directly over his heart and just under his throat, had gone numb. He pinched and poked the spot and felt no pain, no sensation at all. The second spot was just under his sternum. The third was just above his pubic patch. He found the fourth spot at the middle of his lower back, and the fifth several inches above. All five were exactly the same diameter.

Frank sprayed the suds away and had a closer look. There was no discoloration. He stepped out of the shower and examined his backside in the mirror. He pressed the dead spot at the center of his lower back, searching for a lump or pain hidden deep in muscle, and found nothing, felt nothing.

He quickly dried off. It was like parts of him were simply not there.

Frank put on his bathrobe, cinched the waist too tight. He'd never been sick in his life. He'd had colds, but nothing serious. He opened the door to his studio, tugged the shades to let in the light.

He found his phone under a pile of drawings, dialed his doctor's office, and spoke with the receptionist, Carl. He described his symptoms and Carl said, "I have a slot open with Dr. Peel three weeks from tomorrow."

"Can't you get me in sooner?"

"Not unless someone cancels."

"Does that ever happen?"

"No, sir."

"Can I see one of the other doctors?"

"I apologize."

"I'm afraid this might be pretty serious. There's absolutely nothing you can do?"

"What I can do," Carl said, "is send you a helpful brochure filled with valuable information on maintaining a safe and healthy lifestyle."

"No. I don't want a brochure." Frank raised his voice, "I already have fifty of the damned things," and threw the phone.

Frank had done the graphic design work for Dr. Peel's brochures and still had scores of them lying around his studio. He'd been asked to redo the drawings seven times. Forced to produce a hundred whimsical sketches. Happy couples riding bicycles, children swimming, white-haired men playing golf, bunches of fruit, dinner plates filled with greens, bowls of overflowing rainbow pasta, women power-walking, and young boys passing ball, and so many smiling nurses and listening doctors, all rendered in sickening pastels.

Frank gathered up the brochures, crushed them in his fists, and stuffed them in the trash.

Satisfied, he turned on the stereo and got to work on his current project. A local theater was producing an opera and they'd hired him to design the programs and the promotional materials.

Frank settled in at his workstation, flicked on the monitor, and brought up a folder containing preliminary sketches. Frank had not heard of the opera before he was hired and knew little about it. The production company was very specific about what they'd wanted, so there was no reason for him to make any effort to see a taped production. He made a larger profit when a job didn't require research.

And he had no real interest. He couldn't see himself spending three hours sitting through something with a title like *Demon Purse*.

Besides, it seemed like he remembered someone telling him it was a musical comedy. And Frank hated musical comedy.

Chapter 2

Frank missed.

A patch of grass flipped into the air.

"Son of a—"

Frank cursed and stomped. He looked down at the dimpled ball and it tumbled off the tee. He closed his eyes and gripped the leather of his club. He leaned forward, defeated.

"Strike two," Steve said. Steve was Frank's brother. He finished his beer and stepped out of the cart. "Grab those divots and let's go."

Frank didn't answer. He didn't bend to patch the tee.

Steve slid his driver from his bag. He looked down at the divots and then up at Frank. "What the hell are you doing?"

"I haven't been sleeping." Frank's shoulders lost their anger. He hated telling Steve about his health. Steve was a pharmacist and loved to recommend medication. "Three hours is all I'm getting. Sometimes less."

"Why didn't you say something?" Steve adjusted his sun visor and squinted at Frank. "I've got a bottle of metacaffeine tabs in the car. You could've taken one before we started."

"I don't need metas." Frank gestured for Steve to go first and stepped aside. He slung his club over his shoulder. "I don't have any trouble staying awake. I need something to help me sleep."

"Serapuems," Steve stepped up to the tee. He planted his feet. "I've got some back at the house."

"Serapuems?" Frank sat down in the cart and pressed a cool can of beer to his forehead. "I've never heard of it."

"Serapuemide. It's new." Steve re-planted his feet, adjusted his stance, and swung the club. "Works great." His eyes followed the ball down the fairway. "Doesn't leave you feeling groggy in the morning."

The ball bounced three times and landed in a bunker.

"Look what you made me do, Frank." Steve shook his head. "You had my mind on drugs when it should've been on the ball." He wiped the sweat from his brow and turned to look at Frank.

Frank was staring off in the opposite direction of the fairway.

"Frank."

Frank didn't answer.

Steve tapped the side of the cart with his club. "Let's go."

Frank started. "What?"

"It's your turn."

"Oh." Frank turned back around and stared off.

"You don't like golf, do you?"

Frank didn't turn to face the question. "Not really."

"Then why do you come out with me every Sunday morning?"

"I don't know, I need the exercise."

"If you need the exercise, take a walk. I could get a tee time with someone who likes the game."

Frank stepped out of the cart and over to the tee.

"Now, when did you say your doctor could get you in?" Steve cracked open another beer.

Frank took his time answering. He bent over and placed his ball on the tee. His movements were slow and deliberate. "Not for another week."

"You know, I graduated with Buddy Peel. I could call him and get you in sooner."

"No, no." Frank sized up his shot. "I don't want you

15

calling the Banana."

"They don't call him that anymore."

"Didn't he get in trouble for touching people? I mean, back in high school."

Steve laughed. "I don't think so."

"I'm pretty sure he did."

"Then I guess he gets paid to do it now."

Frank swung and missed. He shielded his eyes and watched the divot tumble through the air as if it were a ball sailing true.

Chapter 3

Emaciated celebrity faces stared out at him from inside the glossy tabloid magazine. Frank flipped through page after page of famous people posing outside movie premieres and charity auctions. The gods and goddesses of the silver screen reduced to human dimensions in the eye of the unrefined tabloid photographer. Without the make-up and special effects, they looked like high school teachers, overdressed chaperones at a senior prom.

The faces were familiar, but Frank could only put a name to a half dozen. He didn't bother to read any of the captions as he waited to be called back to the examination room. The social lives of people he would never meet held little interest. But the pictures somehow fascinated him. The sunken cheeks and frail, stick arms of the Hollywood elite. He was particularly struck by the way so many low-cut evening gowns revealed bony chests instead of voluptuous cleavage.

"Frank," the receptionist called, "you can come back now."

Frank folded the magazine in half and followed a nurse to the scale and weighed in.

"You've lost a few pounds since your last visit," the nurse said, jotting a note in his chart.

"My appetite hasn't been the same for the past two weeks."

The nurse nodded, added another quick note, and then escorted him to examination room number three.

She took his temperature, his blood pressure, and asked

him to describe his symptoms. She took more notes and didn't ask for any elaboration. "Okay," she said, looking up with a smile. "Dr. Peel will be with you shortly."

Frank waited thirty minutes. The celebrities made boring company.

"I should've picked up a new magazine," Frank said to himself. "I've been through this one five times."

His attention was drawn from the premiere photos to the ads at the back of the magazine. Cigarettes and bottles of liquor promised the world. He read the classifieds straight through and discovered at least twenty competing diets and weight loss pills, and twice as many exercise machines available to the overweight and unglamorous, all endorsed by some celebrity's personal trainer.

The examination room door opened and the Banana walked in.

But he wasn't called that anymore. He was Dr. Peel now.

He read while he walked, flipping through Frank's chart.

Frank closed his magazine and set it aside, cleared his throat.

"I apologize for the wait," Dr. Peel said. "What are you reading there?"

"Nothing good." Frank flipped the magazine over and pretended to read its title for the first time. "Real Paparazzi. Weekly."

Dr. Peel sat on a stool, retrieved a pen from his coat pocket, depressed the button-top, and jotted something in the margins, smiling down at the paper. He hadn't once looked at Frank since entering the room.

"Spots," Dr. Peel said. "Let's have a look."

"On my chest and on my back."

Dr. Peel looked up, eyes not meeting Frank's, and said, "Take off your shirt."

Frank felt the Banana—

Buddy

Dr. Peel

18

—staring at his throat.

Frank shrugged off his shirt. He pointed to the center of his chest. "Here's one." His fingers moved a few inches down. "Number Two." And he proceeded to point to each spot in the order of its discovery.

"You have no sensation at any of these points?"

"No."

The Banana reached out and touched Frank's chest. He tapped and poked.

"You don't feel that?"

"I don't."

The Banana pinched.

"How about that?"

"Nothing."

The Banana pinched harder. "That?"

"Nope."

The Banana frowned and pinched Frank's right nipple.

"Ouch. What are you doing?"

"Good." Dr. Peel turned away to take notes. "No discoloration. And I didn't find anything hidden in deeper tissue. We'll have to take samples, of course." The Banana slapped Frank on the knee. "That shouldn't be a problem for you. You'll save some money, since we can skip the local anesthetic."

The Banana reached between Frank's legs and opened a drawer in the examination table. He reached inside and unwrapped a sterile pouch. He ripped the seal and four tiny instruments tumbled out onto a stainless steel tray, like drug paraphernalia made for squirrels. Syringe and a drawing bottle, sample vial, and razor-spoon.

Dr. Peel took the sample vial in one hand and the razor-spoon in the other and stood up.

"Lie down," he said. "And are you sure you don't want me to use the anesthetic?"

"I haven't turned it down."

"But you shouldn't need it."

"I suppose not," Frank said, lying down. "And if it does hurt, then we've learned something, right?"

"Yeah. Right." The Banana placed his left hand on Frank's chest. The sample vial was cold and puckered his skin. Dr. Peel cocked his head, bit his lip, and held his instrument high, delicately, between his thumb and forefinger. He charted his course, nodded, muttered something under his breath, then swooped down and made his incision.

Frank felt nothing. The doctor jerked forward and the next thing Frank noticed was the tinkling sound of the razor-spoon depositing its load into the sample vial.

"That didn't hurt at all?" Dr. Peel asked.

"You're finished?"

"Would you mind if I took a sample from the remainder of the affected areas?"

"Will this leave scars?"

"Shouldn't. But I can give you something. I've got samples lying around. I'm sure."

"Okay, then. Go ahead."

Frank expected to see the man suddenly rubbing his hands together with greedy anticipation.

The Banana dug out and patched four more little holes in Frank's torso, and labeled the samples, coding them according to their source location on the body.

"That's good." Dr. Peel corked the last vial and wiped the spoon clean. "We still have a healthy blood flow in the affected areas." He turned and washed his hands in the sink. "There was quite a mess."

Frank groaned as he sat up. He fingered the bandages on his torso. The discount medical tape tugged at his chest hair.

"What do you think this is?" Frank asked.

"Don't know," said Dr. Peel, re-arranging his samples on the tray. "This is going to take some research."

"You've never seen anything like this before?"

"Not exactly like it. No."

"But you've seen similar conditions?"

Dr. Peel nodded.

"Well, what conditions?"

Dr. Peel frowned and shook his head. "You're right, I haven't seen anything like it. Like I said, it will take some research. We'll schedule more tests while we wait for the tissue to come back from the labs."

"What kind of tests?"

"Nothing intrusive." Dr. Peel waved his hand. "I'll just want a bunch of pictures ordered. I was recently certified at Springbrook Regional Hospital, and they've got a new state-of-the-art imaging facility there. They really have gotten the radiation levels down on these new machines."

Chapter 4

"Keep absolutely still, all the way through the procedure." Dr. Peel adjusted dials and entered information through the machine's keyboard. "And like with any other imaging device, you want to make double-y sure that you don't move while you're inside the cylinder."

"What if I have to sneeze?" Frank asked, legs together, arms pressed tight to his sides. "What happens if I *do* move?"

"Don't."

"I won't. I just want to know what would happen if I did."

Dr. Peel switched on a desk lamp and studied an operator's manual.

"What could happen?" Frank asked. He didn't like being ignored.

"Hmmm," Dr. Peel said. "What? Oh, I'm not sure what would happen with this one. I've never used this particular device before. I'm sure whatever happens, it's not good. But it's probably much better than the earlier imagers."

"What happened in the older models?"

"If you moved while inside the cylinder?"

"Yes."

"Well." Dr. Peel stood and wiped lint from his trousers. He walked over to Frank and strapped him to the insertion platform. "If you moved in the old T-SCAN devices, the imaging lasers would slice you into a dozen pieces. The lasers on this one would probably just burn you."

Frank struggled against his restraints. "Are you serious?"

"No," Dr. Peel said. "'Imaging lasers?' Come on, Frank. I made that up. I really have no idea what happens if you move while you're inside one of these things. It probably just messes the pictures up. You won't find any airplane propellers in there, if that's what you're worried about."

Frank relaxed a bit. He took a deep breath, closed his eyes, and tried to tell himself that he wasn't claustrophobic.

"Are you ready?" Dr. Peel asked.

"How long will I have to be in there?"

"Just a few minutes." The doctor walked behind a protective shield and took his seat before the controls. "And you don't have to close your eyes, Frank. No flashing bulbs."

Frank waited in darkness and listened to flicking switches, to the doctor flipping pages in his manual.

Finally, the insertion platform hummed to life and Frank was drawn into the mouth of the imaging cylinder. His naked skin tingled. He pictured the fine hairs on his arms and legs standing on end. It was cold inside the machine.

Frank remained perfectly still for over thirty minutes before he was finally drawn out again into the dry hospital air. Frank breathed out and opened his eyes. "I thought you said it would only take a few minutes?"

Dr. Peel didn't answer. Frank didn't hear papers shuffling, any pencil scratching.

"Are you there?" Frank called out.

Dr. Peel's voice came a moment later. "What? What was that you said?"

"Didn't you say this would only take a few minutes."

"I decided to take some additional pictures." Dr. Peel stood up and stretched. He groaned as if he'd just woken from a pleasant nap. "I didn't realize that this thing had so many options. I had to try them all."

"How many additional pictures?" Frank asked. This was beginning to sound expensive. He didn't like the idea of paying extra money just to satisfy this man's intellectual curiosity.

"Just a few hundred."

"How many?"

"Just over three hundred."

"That can't be necessary." Frank tried to sit up. The plastic restraints pinched his skin.

"Not absolutely necessary," Dr. Peel said. "No."

"Would you mind getting me out of these straps?"

Dr. Peel stepped from behind the shield-wall and unsnapped buckles.

"How much is all this going to cost me?" Frank asked. "Three hundred sounds a bit excessive."

"It won't be too bad. They're really pushing this device nowadays. I get the first few thousand snapshots at a reduced rate. Admittedly, I did go a bit overboard. So, I don't mind passing the savings down to you."

The doctor patted Frank's arm. "Come on. Hop up. The best thing about this machine is that the images are developed instantly. I really can't wait to see these."

· · · · · ·

Frank dressed and walked into the screening room. Dr. Peel was already standing in front of an over-sized monitor, flipping through images of what Frank assumed were detailed cross-sections of his body. They looked like elaborate, ultraviolet Rorschach blotters. He saw faces in his internal organs, ant colonies in his veins, storm clouds in the folds of his brain tissue.

"These are great images, huh, Frank?" Dr. Peel didn't turn to acknowledge Frank's presence. The swirling vortices of Frank's interior transfixed him.

"Finding anything?" Frank asked.

Dr. Peel pressed a button on a remote control and flipped through a series of pictures before answering.

"Uh, no. Hold on." A dozen more images flashed by. "I'll be with you in a minute."

Frank watched the man's face as he examined the

images. He detected a boyhood joy beneath the colored shadows splashing across his features.

"You're not much of a gadget man, are you, Frank?"

"What do you mean?"

"You're not into gadgets? Pocket computers? The latest phones?"

"No."

"I'm a gadget man. That's why I'm probably the only doctor in the country who's gone through the trouble getting certified to run these imagers. I've got to have the car alarms and the electric toothbrush. I'm almost obsessive about electric razors. Always have to have the newest models. I have one of those with the vacuum built in. It sucks up the hair as you go. My wife's happy not to see the little hairs all over the sink."

"I don't have an electric razor," Frank said. "It just feels like the safety razors give you a closer shave."

"You're wrong there," Dr. Peel said, face glowing with wonder as hundreds of splices of Frank's body flashed by on the screen. "This new one is great, with the vacuum. It gets as close—"

"Excuse me. But are you finding anything?"

"Oh, I'm not looking. I mean, I finished looking a few minutes ago. I wasn't able to find anything at all. Everything looks good."

"What now?"

"We wait." Dr. Peel switched off the monitor. "We'll have the results from the tissue scan in a few days. We should know more at that time."

"When are those tests due back, again?"

The Banana put his hand on Frank's shoulder and guided him out to the waiting room. "Don't stay up worrying about it, Frank. My office will call you with the results when they come in."

"When should that be, exactly?"

"A few days." Dr. Peel escorted Frank through the

automatic doors and out to the sidewalk. He waved to Frank as the doors drew closed, calling after him, "It could be a week. Maybe two."

Chapter 5

A boy and a girl held hands on a park bench. Their eyes were closed. Their lips were puckered. They sat frozen in place, about to share a first kiss, dressed in their Sunday best. The boy wore a rumpled suit and the girl a spring dress with a matching yellow handbag. Blurry trees and fuzzy green grass surrounded them. A family of pigeons pecked at the sidewalk. And above their heads, scrawled in formal script, were the words *Demon Purse*.

Frank sat back in his chair, crossed his arms over his chest, and stared at this image on the monitor. He considered for a moment and clicked his mouse.

Horns sprouted from the children's foreheads.

Frank clicked the mouse again and the horns disappeared.

The phone rang and Frank swiveled in his chair to answer it.

"This is Carl," the voice on the other end said.

"Who?" Frank asked.

The line was silent.

"Are you there? Hello?"

Frank heard a deep inhalation and then, "It's Carl."

"Yes?"

"From Dr. Peel's office?"

"Oh, sorry." Frank had no idea why he was apologizing.

"That's okay," Carl said.

Frank waited for Carl to continue. He dialed down his stereo, turned his back to his computer screen. "Are you there?"

"Yes."

"What can I do for you, Carl?"

"I was calling with your test results."

Frank flipped his mouse over and unscrewed the bottom. He removed the batteries and rolled them between his palms. He waited and waited for Carl to continue, but then grew tired of waiting.

"And?" Frank asked.

"That's it," Carl said. "I just called to give you the test results."

"And what were they?"

"They didn't find nothing."

"They found nothing?"

"That's what I said."

"No, it's not," Frank said, but decided not to press the point. He didn't want to start an argument with Carl. "When can I come back in?"

"Are you sick?"

"What do you mean?"

"What are your symptoms?"

"The spots."

"The spots? Why would you come back for that?"

"Because they're still there."

"But Dr. Peel said there is nothing wrong with you. The tests turned up nothing."

"So, that's it?"

Frank heard Carl flipping through his chart. "The tests show that there is nothing physically wrong with you."

"No more tests are scheduled?"

"No."

"Dr. Peel is just giving up?"

"No. I wouldn't call it that. He ran tests and—"

"I know." Frank sighed. "Well, does he think it's psychological then?"

"That's what it says," Carl said, rustling pages, "at the bottom here."

"So, does the doctor have a referral for me?"

"Yes, you have an appointment with Dr. Vo on the twenty-fifth."

"Can you ask the doctor if he can refer me to someone else?"

Dr. Vo was the only psychiatrist in town, and he had a reputation. The man had divorced his wife and was now living with a former patient twenty years his junior.

"He's the only doctor in your plan for this geographical area. That's the best we can do. Unless you want to drive to Spring City to see someone else?"

"That's the closest?

"That's the closest."

"No. I can't do that."

"The twenty-fifth," Carl said.

"What time on the twenty-fifth?"

Frank received no answer.

"Carl? Hello?"

The line was dead.

Chapter 6

Frank was going to a party. He shaved, showered, and put on fresh clothes. He pulled open a clear Mylar bag, reached inside and pulled out a cheap plastic mask. He stretched its rubber-band over his head and let it snap against the back of his skull.

Frank drove slowly to his brother's house, hoping to pass someone on the streets. He wanted to see a reaction to his mask. But he didn't see a single car out on the road.

The only person he saw was a young girl riding a bicycle, but she went past him and around a corner so fast that he wasn't sure that she had noticed him. Frank had even stuck his masked face out the window at her, made an effort to see her expression, but he wasn't able to make out her features. Her face was oddly flat and pasty. He imagined her eyes, nose, and mouth sliding over her chin and onto her dress.

Frank turned the car around and followed the girl. He wanted to confirm that what he had just seen was indeed a hallucination. He turned the wheel and the corner just in time to see the girl roll up into a driveway. She dropped her bike behind a black sedan and ran inside the open garage. Frank was only able to catch another quick glimpse of her face, her cheek, as she turned away. He saw only blurred skin, no depth, no nose, no color, and no eyes. The garage door closed and Frank sped up as he passed the house.

He tried to shake the faceless girl from his mind as he turned around and headed back toward Steve's. He looked into the rear-view mirror and ran his fingers through his hair. He had a vision of himself, an hour into the future, surrounded by masked strangers. His hair was wet in this vision and he didn't know why. But his imagined future self went on slicking his hair back anyway, tight to his head, charged with an odd, grimy sense of superiority.

Frank pulled the car to the curb and walked up the steps to Steve's porch. He knocked on the screen door. Bodies moved in shadow across drawn shades.

Steve's wife, Jill, answered the door. Her mask covered almost her entire face. It was silver and did nothing to conceal her pained grin.

"Frank," she said.

"Yes."

"Hold on a minute, Frank. I'll be right back." Jill left the door open a crack and walked away.

Her shadow moved across drawn shades. She stomped over to Steve's shadow, waved her hands, and pointed to the door.

"Hi, Frank," Steve said, poking his head through the screen door. His mask was red, with plastic feather eyebrows. "I'm glad you could make it."

"Is everything all right?" Frank asked. "It didn't seem like Jill was expecting me."

"She wasn't. My fault. You just surprised her, that's all."

"Are you sure?"

"It's nothing personal." Steve lifted his mask and winked. "She's just worried about not having enough food."

"I don't want to cause you any problems." Frank turned and pointed to the street. "I can go."

"No." Steve opened the door. "I'm glad you could make it."

Frank stepped inside. Candelabras flickered in the foyer. He heard laughter, ice tinkling in glasses, echoing down the hallway. Steve led him into the living room and the voices stopped. The party-goers looked at Frank and whispered amongst themselves shamelessly, like schoolgirls.

"Everyone," Steve said, raising his glass to the silence.

"This is my brother, Frank."

No one moved or said a word.

"He's in graphic design."

A woman in a catcher's mask coughed. She leaned in close to her date and whispered something in his ear, looking at Frank the entire time. She sat with her legs tucked up under her on the couch. Her skirt was bunched up around her waist. Her garter belt and stockings matched exactly the color of her skin.

Her date wore a black satin robe with a hood. His mask had a pig's snout and slanted eyes. He sipped his drink and nodded as he listened to his date's whispers.

Frank moved his eyes from the stockings to a broad coffee table. A miniature city of wineglasses and half-finished bottles of wine towered over candy trays filled with multicolored pills and tablets. A gum ball machine stood with civic pride as the centerpiece, its geodesic glass sphere filled with half-blue, half-purple capsules.

Steve nudged Frank's arm. He nodded to the pharmaceutical metropolis and said, "It's not quite as extravagant as it looks. The gum ball machine is mostly filler, over-the-counter painkillers. If you want anything, just ask someone what it is before you take it. Almost everyone here is a pharmacist or a doctor."

"I'll remember that." *Because I'm sure they won't let me forget it.* Frank turned away from the crowd in search of a drink.

"Scotch?" Steve asked.

Frank followed Steve to an ancient, baroque dining table, its base a charging bull carved from a great mahogany block. This makeshift bar served as a neighboring city, a megalopolis of silver and glass, of polished decanters and shining jiggers, dark bottles of gleaming liqueur, sparkling trays of fruit, meat, and cheese.

Steve was nudging Frank again.

"It's a rental," he said. "Jill would never allow such a thing as a permanent fixture in her home."

"I wasn't going to say anything," Frank said.

"I know. It's a little over the top."

Steve packed a glass full of ice with a pair of gaudy metal tongs. Its pincers were clapping angel wings.

"Where do you even rent such a thing?" Frank asked, stepping back from the table, peering underneath at the rippling, muscled wood.

"There's a place out in California called *Events*." Steve tipped a bottle of whiskey into the glass. "They have all kinds of great stuff. There's a catalog around here somewhere. Remind me later, I'll find it for you."

"You shipped this thing all the way from California?"

"I am a drug dealer." Steve finished building the drink with a smile. "It's good to see you out."

"Yeah."

Steve handed over the Scotch.

Frank sucked down half of it and held out his glass for a refill. The glass looked like a rental, too, lead crystal, etched with dancing ivy and tangled nymphs.

"Whatever happened with that opera gig?" Steve asked. "You ever hear anything back?"

"Yeah. I already started working on it."

"You did?"

"Couple of weeks ago."

"You should have told me. I would have bought you a drink."

"Come on."

"It's the biggest job you've had in a while. It could turn into an annual thing."

"I don't know."

"The city's throwing money at that opera house these days. Part of their big five year urban renewal initiative."

"It's bullshit."

"Yeah. But why not cash in on the bullshit while you can?"

"Excuse me." Frank took the bottle from Steve's hands

and replenished his Scotch. "I've got to go to the restroom."

Steve sipped his drink, nodded toward the hallway. "You know where it is."

· · · · · ·

Frank zipped up and turned to the sink to wash his hands. He found the liquid-soap pump dry and turned in circles in search of an alternative. He drew the shower curtain and spotted a bar of soap across the wide Jacuzzi tub. He had to bend over and really reach to grab hold of the slippery shell-shaped thing. The shower nozzle drizzled on his head, water dribbled down the inside of his shirt.

Frank washed up and returned the soap to the dish. He grabbed the doorknob before drying his hands and his hand slipped, opening the bathroom door.

He heard voices coming from the bedroom across the hall, angry whispers.

"Keep your voice down," Steve said. "He's in there taking a piss."

Frank pushed the door, almost closed it, after hearing this. He pulled the hand towel from the rack and listened more closely while drying his hands.

"I can't believe you asked him here for this," Jill said. "It's not happening with him. If that's what you're after. He's your fucking brother."

"Half-brother. Technically."

"It's still fucking sick."

Steve laughed.

"I just wanted to see the guy around people for a change. He's not going to stay that late, I can tell you that. It's obvious he's uncomfortable."

"He better not stay all night."

"I can't believe you'd think I would ask you to do something like that."

"I don't know with you sometimes, Steve."

"Come on."

34

"You are the creep who got me into this."

"Creep!" Steve said in a voice belonging to a low-rent cartoon vampire.

Jill giggled and Frank heard sickening kisses, a playful struggle.

Frank slowly hung the towel on the rack, listening carefully for the sound of footsteps returning to the party, and seriously considered making a run for the front door.

Steve and Jill shuffled past the bathroom in short bursts, pushing each other like fighting siblings.

Frank counted to thirty before he dared to open the door and stepped into the hall.

The voices didn't stop when he entered the living room for the second time, and he was grateful to be ignored. He returned to the rented bar and fixed himself another Scotch. He sipped and turned to observe the mingling party-goers. They talked quietly in small groups.

A man pointed at pills in the palm of his hand. His date smoked and gave her opinion of each one. In the corner, a couple tangled together, dressed in matching satin military attire, sparkling gold braids, and flashing medals. Their masks were the color of dull tank steel. The eye holes were trimmed with raised plastic rivets.

Frank turned away out of an irrational fear that they would be upset if he'd been caught staring. Steve and Jill were standing a few feet away from the couple. Steve had his shoulders hunched and was gesturing with upturned palms, trying to convince Jill of something, failing in his attempts at discretion. Jill's arms were folded and she shook her head, eyes half-closed. Steve finally threw his arms up in defeat and stomped off to the bar and began moving bottles from the bar top over to the nearby kitchen counter.

Frank at first thought that Jill had given the order to end the party early. But when he looked around to gauge the reactions on the faces surrounding him, he found eager smiles and nods of approval.

A shirtless man, wearing a cowl fastened around his neck with a bow tie, stepped forward and helped Steve clear the table.

Once it was clear, Jill appeared from the kitchen with a rag and a can of furniture polish. She sprayed and wiped the table down. When she was finished, Steve unfurled a red tablecloth and covered the table.

A woman dressed in overalls and a mask covered with leaves and plastic birds handed her glass to her date and performed a cartwheel, which ended gracefully with her feet planted on the tabletop. She unsnapped her shoulder straps and her overalls dropped, revealing flesh and bristly floral negligee.

Frank turned away, embarrassed, and was startled to find the party gathered directly behind him now, standing too close, with big smiles, breathing rhythmically through their noses.

Unsure of himself, he jiggled his glass, and pretended to take great interest in watching the ice sloshing around inside. He sidestepped out of the front row and made his way around to a more comfortable position at the rear of the audience.

The floral negligee was gyrating awkwardly above the tabletop. The woman's face was serious. No music played on the stereo. She pouted, in search of a song lost inside her skull. She raised her hands and crossed her forearms behind her head and began to hum tunelessly to herself.

Frank shook his head, sipped his drink, tried to divert his attention. He was beginning to think that this woman's mental deficiencies were being put on display for everyone's amusement. He looked to the brick fireplace, the plaster walls, the frames filled with simple erotic line drawings. He'd never noticed them before.

Creep. Jill's voice echoed in his memory. Frank nodded his head in agreement. His brother was a creep. Always had been. He was a cad with delusions of good taste. In college, he believed his framed collection of 1940s pin-up girls was the pinnacle of class.

Frank looked back at the floral-print underwear hovering over the tabletop. The flesh beneath the cloth had stopped moving. The girl was staring over the heads of the party-goers. Frank expected a string of drool to start stretching from her bottom lip.

Frank thought she might be depressed and a little hurt, because the party-goers were no longer interested in her. They had turned away and were staring at the wall of sketched nudes.

Creeps.

Frank ran his fingers over his scalp. His hair was wet and he didn't know why.

A man wearing a mask covered with a raised brick pattern walked past Frank to the wall of erotic art. Frank noticed a crack in the wall that he hadn't noticed before, between a woman's dimpled posterior and the whimsical rendering of a nude fairy spying on two human lovers engaged in a forest clearing. The crack grew bigger as Brick Face approached, opening up for him like a hungry Venus Flytrap.

Frank, startled, took a step back and surveyed the party-goers. It was difficult to see their reactions beneath their masks, but he saw no indication that these people thought of this bizarre happening as anything more than just a part of the evening's entertainment.

A small arm poked out from the crack and twisted around in search of something to grab on to. It was an infant's arm with silvery skin. Its wrist and finger joints were held together with plastic bolts. It was a doll's arm, Frank decided, poking in from a side-wise universe populated with gray-skinned people.

Brick Face held his fingers out to the tiny hand and the silver arm twitched and swirled, knocking into Brick Face's wrist violently.

This contact brought on an instant transformation in Brick Face. His mask disappeared, and his costume, a construction worker's uniform covered with stencils of famous architectural triumphs, disappeared and was replaced with a black suit and sequined cape. A top hat sprouted from his skull and a white-tipped magician's wand appeared in his hand.

The party-goers gasped and clapped with delight.

Frank dropped his glass. He looked around, expecting to find Jill staring at him with disgust. But she wasn't paying him any attention. She was focused on the magician. Frank quickly crouched and retrieved the glass, which, thankfully, wasn't broken. Steve's house was lined with the most expensive plush carpet money could buy. Frank picked up his scattered ice cubes and returned them to his glass.

Frank stood. The magician raised his hands and walked through the parted crowd to the table. He reached up and took hold of the floral girl's hand and turned to address his audience.

"Ladies and gentleman," he said with a nasally voice, "I will now perform my first feat of the evening." He pulled the girl toward him and their mouths locked together for a long, salacious kiss.

The audience laughed.

The girl pulled away, smiled, and wiped her mouth. Then the magician, with chivalrous flair, helped her lie down on the table.

Frank had a feeling that he knew what was coming. He remembered Jill and Steve's conversation from earlier in the evening. *It's not happening with him, if that's what you're after.* Frank expected the magician to crawl on top of the table and begin the evening's orgy with a duet performance. A little warm-up to get everyone in the mood.

But the magician circled the table instead, arms raised, colorful ribbons firing out of his sleeves.

This was met with more laughter and applause.

The magician yanked the tablecloth out from underneath the girl with a single smooth movement, demonstrating a great degree of showmanship, and draped it over the supine girl. He raised his arms, clapped three times, and snapped the cloth from the table again with equal flourish.

And the girl was gone, replaced with a cheap plastic skeleton, the kind found bobbing on front doors on Halloween night, with a goofy overbite and bulging eyes.

The audience gasped and clapped and clapped.

The magician bowed, flipping the tablecloth from left to right, displaying both sides, like a matador. He then turned and covered the dime-store skeleton, clapped three times, snatched the cloth from the table, and the skeleton was gone.

More applause, more laughter.

"Now, for my next trick," said the magician, "I will need a volunteer."

Next trick?

Frank thought it strange that the magician had no intention of bringing the girl back from whatever void he'd banished her to.

No volunteers stepped forward.

"Don't be frightened," the magician said.

No one moved.

"You there," the magician called, pointing over the first row of heads with his wand. Its white tip pointed directly at Frank. "Step forward and be amazed."

Frank stepped back, shaking his head. "No thanks," he said. He tipped his glass to his lips to have a drink, and his mouth filled with wet carpet fuzz.

"Come on, Frank," Steve said, emerging from the crowd and slinging an arm over his shoulders. "It'll be fun."

Frank picked carpet fuzz off his tongue as Steve pushed him forward through the crowd. Steve planted Frank by the table, plucked his glass from his hand, and retreated to the first row of spectators.

"We have a volunteer," the magician cheered.

Steve laughed and nudged the masked men standing to his left and right.

"My next trick will astonish you," the magician said. "I will just have you lie down, sir."

Frank threw up his hands in protest. "No, I'm sorry, but I really don't think I'm the right person for this. Could you pick somebody else?"

"Sir, you're the perfect subject, Mister…Mister?" the magician asked.

"Frank."

"You'll do just fine, Mr. Frank." The magician placed a calming hand on Frank's shoulder and nudged him backward toward the table.

Jill called out from near the back of the crowd, "Be a sport."

Her sentiments were matched with a chorus of agreement, nodding heads, and impatient whispers.

Frank didn't feel like he had a choice. He sat down on the table and the magician poked him in the chest with his wand, pushing him back to a reclining position.

"Don't worry, Mr. Frank," he said. "I only kiss my female assistants."

More laughter.

Frank felt blood rush to his face. He didn't like being the center of attention, the source of amusement. He was angry, but he tried to remain calm. It was too late to back out now.

His little part of the show would be over soon enough.

The magician made three passes with his wand over Frank's body, from head to toe, from toe to head. With each pass, Frank felt more relaxed. And with the final pass, he felt his muscles liquefy, a heavy paralysis setting in. He tried to move his limbs, to wriggle his toes, and discovered that he no longer had control over his own body.

Frank was terrified. He didn't like losing control. He

struggled to move, to right himself, to sit up and jump from the table, run out the front door and into the streets. But he was trapped. His flesh felt like three hundred pounds of wet cement poured over helpless bones. He tried to open his mouth to scream, to plead for release, but his tongue was dead. His jaw was limp and useless.

"Ladies and gentlemen," the magician said, "prepare to be astonished!"

The magician circled the table and Frank heard a distant clanging sound, like a truckload of pipes rolling down a hillside.

The magician raised his right arm straight over his head and a pipe rose out of his sleeve. It performed a sleepy dance, like a hypnotized cobra. The magician took the pipe in hand and twirled it like a baton. The pipe was about three feet in length and hollow. It sang as it was whipped through the air.

"Now this won't hurt a bit," the magician said. He took the pipe in both hands and impaled Frank's lower abdomen.

Frank would have jumped, would have screamed, if he could. But he was helpless. He could feel the pipe pass through him, but it wasn't painful. The magician had been telling the truth. It didn't hurt a bit. He felt instead a tugging sensation, like the terrible discomfort he'd suffered years ago when his doctor had sent a camera up his ass to inspect his small intestines.

Although there was no pain, there was blood. As soon as one end of the pipe was lodged into his gut, a splash of red burst from the opposite end. But instead of dribbling down the length of the pipe and onto the table, the crimson burst stayed fixed in the air, as if time had suddenly stopped. And then Frank realized that what he saw wasn't blood, but a bouquet of red roses pushed up through the end of the pipe.

The crowd went wild.

The magician threw his wand into the air and it spun like

a propeller over Frank's face, defying gravity for an incredible length of time, before it dropped again into the magician's hand, transformed into a second length of pipe. The magician raised the pipe and drove it through Frank's solar plexus.

Frank felt the uncomfortable tugging again. And this time he noticed the crunch of the pipe penetrating the wood at his back.

Or was that the snapping of my spine?

Frank stopped breathing.

Lotus blossoms sprung from the top of the pipe.

More applause.

The magician reached up and plucked the roses from the first pipe and presented them to a woman standing in the front row. She blushed, gloated over her prize to her neighbors.

The magician returned to the pipe, waved his hands, and his wand was returned to him. It shot up from inside the pipe as if borne by a tightly coiled spring. The magician caught it and followed up with a grandiloquent bow.

He then plucked the lotus blossoms from the second pipe and tossed them to another woman standing near the back of the gathering. She yelped with surprise and giggled with embarrassment as she fumbled to catch the bouquet.

The magician called for absolute quiet. When all was still, he performed a variety of arcane gesticulations over the second pipe. And a third pipe telescoped from within, jumping into his hands. The magician twirled it overhead, turning in circles like a go-go cowgirl twirling a lasso in just her bra and panties, and then drove the third and final pipe straight through Frank's chest.

Chapter 7

Frank clutched his chest, sweating. Tears ran down his cheeks. His clothes were a mess. He twisted and writhed on Dr. Vo's leather chase lounge.

Dr. Vo reached out a calming hand and gripped Frank's shoulder. "It's over now, Frank? Is that the end of the dream?"

"Yes," Frank said. "It's over. I'm dead."

"You're not dead, Frank. It was just a dream. Let's begin the calming exercises I taught you. Remember?"

"Yes."

Dr. Vo guided Frank through a series of rhythmic breathing techniques, and soon Frank's chest rose and fell with a steady, even cadence. The tears stopped flowing and his arms fell away to his sides.

"Good, Frank. You're doing great. That was a very traumatic dream. I can understand why you suppressed it. Reliving something like that is tough. But you did very well."

"Thank you."

"Now, I want you to relax, and I'll bring you back to the office, OK?"

"OK."

"In just a moment, I will begin counting floors. You understand what I mean by that?"

"Yes. You will count backwards through the levels of consciousness until we reach the top."

"Correct. After which, you will be totally awake and aware."

"Yeah."

"But first I would like to ask you a few questions."

"OK."

"Frank, have you had this dream before?"

"I don't think so."

"Think back."

"No. That was the first time. I'm certain of it."

"Was the magician someone you recognized from real life?"

"No. I've never seen him before."

"Was he a composite?"

"I don't know…"

"Were his features a combination of two or more people you do know? Think, Frank."

Frank concentrated and shook his head. "No."

"OK, Frank. Very good. I'm going to begin counting levels in a second. First, I want to lay down some ground rules. When you wake up, you will remember the entire contents of your dream, but you are forbidden to feel anxious about it. It's just a dream. OK?"

"OK."

"Secondly. Now this part you won't remember when you wake up, me telling you this. Trust me, it's for the better. Secondly, I want you to buy my book, *Dealing with Yourself*. It just came out in paperback. When you leave my office today, I want you to go directly to the nearest bookstore and pick up a copy. Are you comfortable with that?"

"Yeah, I guess so."

"Great. I think you'll find it illuminating."

Dr. Vo retrieved a metronome from his desk and set it down on the coffee table across from Frank. He twisted a knob on its back and set it into motion. He sat down in the chair opposite Frank and counted backwards, slowly, in time with the beat, from twenty to one.

"Take a deep breath, Frank. We're back."

Frank's chest heaved and his eyes opened. He turned his head, looked at Dr. Vo, and let loose a sigh of relief.

"How do you feel?"

"Awake," Frank said. "More awake than I've felt in days. Well-rested."

"Relieved?"

Frank furrowed his brow. "Yeah, I do feel relieved. Like I just survived a bad car wreck without a scratch."

"You survived the dream, Frank. You do remember?"

Frank sat up and threw his legs over the side of the couch. He looked at the doctor, cocked his head, and began unbuttoning his shirt.

"What's going on, Frank?"

Frank shrugged his shirt off, pulled his undershirt up over his head, and stood with his back to the doctor.

"I can't reach back there. Would you mind?"

"What?"

"I want you to jab me in the back with something. I think we've found my sixth dead spot."

"I'm sure we have, Frank." Dr. Vo stood and poked Frank in the back with his index finger. "You feel that?"

"Yes. Move up and over a bit. It should match up exactly with the spot on my chest."

"There?" Dr. Vo asked.

"What?"

"There. Can you feel that?"

"No."

"That's it then. You sure you don't feel anything?"

"Nothing."

"Just a minute, Frank."

Dr. Vo went to his desk and grabbed a paper-clip. He unwound it and tested its point on the tip of his finger. He returned to Frank and stabbed it into Frank's back.

Frank didn't flinch. "What are you up to back there?"

"You didn't feel that either?"

"No."

"Hmm," Dr. Vo said. "Hold still for a moment. I need to clean up."

"Clean up?"

"Get a bandage and some antiseptic. It won't take a minute."

"What? You just stabbed me? I said 'jab.'"

"Just a necessary test. Don't worry."

"What did you stab me with?"

"An instrument I had on hand."

Frank turned around and scanned the room. His eyes settled on the misshapen paper-clip on Vo's desk.

"Paper-clips are considered medical instruments these days?"

Dr. Vo laughed. "They'll do in a pinch. Turn back around."

Frank turned around and waited while Dr. Vo cleaned and bandaged his sixth dead spot.

"What do you think all this means?"

"I'm not exactly sure. But we'll figure it out."

"Have you ever seen anything like this before?"

"Not personally, no. But I do seem to remember reading about a few cases similar to this. I'll have to dig up some journals, do a little homework. They weren't exactly like your case. But they did involve psychosomatic diseases, diseases the subjects believed they had contracted while in dreams."

Frank pulled his undershirt back over his head. "Were they curable?"

"Oh, I'm sure they were." Dr. Vo sat down at his desk and began scribbling on a yellow legal pad. "I have a feeling that your symptoms will disappear in time, now that your conscious mind knows their source."

"I hope so."

"Now, figuring out the 'why' of your traumatic dream may take a little longer. We have some work to do. How do you feel about weekly visits until we get this all straightened out?"

"I don't know. I'm self-employed. The co-pay on top of the premiums would set me back quite a bit."

"We can work with you there, Frank, put you on a payment plan. It is important to you that we get past this?"

"Yeah." Frank looked down at his shirt, watching his hands work the buttons. "You're right."

Dr. Vo stabbed a spot at the bottom of his legal pad and slashed his pen across the bottom of the page, underlining something. He then slid open a drawer and the pad disappeared inside. He pulled out a smaller yellow pad from the drawer and began filling out a prescription. "I'm going to give you something to help you sleep."

"All right," Frank said. Then he thought of his dire financial situation again. "Wait. What are you giving me?"

"Serapuems."

"They're new, aren't they?"

"Yes. How'd you know that?"

"My brother, he's a pharmacist, he swears by them."

"They're the best I've seen yet. They induce the most restful sleep without any of the next-day grogginess associated with so many other sleep aides."

"Well, Doc, I hate to ask you this. But, considering they are new to the market, I know that the distributors like to promote their wares—"

"You want to know if I have any samples lying around?"

"Yeah. Like I said, money is tight right now. I am about to finish a job here in the next few weeks. But until then, I'm just barely scraping by."

"No problem. Just ask the receptionist on the way out. I'll tell her to give you a box."

"I appreciate it."

"Our time's just about up. What do you say? Same time next week?"

"Sure."

"One more thing." Dr. Vo stood, grabbed Frank's shoulder and shook his hand. "I'd like to make a recommendation."

"You want me to lay off the Scotch?"

Dr. Vo laughed. "No. Although, that wouldn't be a bad idea.

"No. I was just going to tell you that I have a new book out in paperback. Only a few bucks. I think you might find it helpful. It's called *Dealing with Yourself*. It's available at most chains."

"OK." Frank dropped Dr. Vo's hand and turned to leave.

"Just thought I'd put that out there," Dr. Vo said. "Keep it in mind, Frank. It's not a prescription, merely a suggestion."

Chapter 8

The cream had gone bad and there was no sugar, so Frank had his coffee black. He shuffled from the kitchen, still in his robe, to the studio and flipped on the light. Sketch books and loose paper covered the floor. Tubes and brushes lay scattered over TV trays. Finished panels teetered precariously on easels throughout the space.

Frank went to the closet and retrieved his portfolio binder, cleared an empty spot on his workbench with a sweep of the arm, unzipped the binder and lay it open.

He looked down at the pile he'd swept from the bench to make sure he hadn't broken anything or displaced something of value. He found Dr. Vo's book resting on the top of the pile. Its corners were worn, but not from reading. The thing had been kicked and thrown around the room for three weeks.

Frank had no idea why he'd even bought the damned thing. He had no intention of reading it. It was written in a cloying self-help tone, and Frank hated self-help books.

Frank had no idea why he still went to see Dr. Vo. The Serapuems were helping though. He couldn't remember ever sleeping so soundly in his life. But the pills did nothing to stop the dream. If anything, they made things worse. Now that Frank's conscious mind could remember the dream, his sleeping mind just wouldn't let him stop dreaming it. He started each morning now remembering Steve's party with vivid detail. The doll's silver hand and the magician stayed with him until noon.

Frank kicked *Dealing with Yourself* in the corner and

buried it in a pile of trash, wishing he'd never admitted to Dr. Vo that he'd bought the thing. He was tired of making up reasons why he hadn't gotten around to reading it yet.

Frank checked the time on the clear plastic desk clock and cursed himself for procrastinating once again. The clock read 12:15, which meant that it was nearly 12:30, and he had be downtown at the opera house to make his presentation at 2 o'clock. He should have assembled the work for the Springville Opera job in his portfolio the night before. But he had been too drunk and too tired, up all night debating with himself on how long he had to wait after his last beer before daring to take his nightly dose of Serapuemide. He had waited until nearly 5 AM before deciding just to take half a tablet. And he was surprised now that he didn't feel groggy on only six hours sleep.

Frank flipped on his stereo and cranked the volume in an attempt to drown out his thoughts. He didn't want to think about bad habits and a shaky work ethic, and he had a feeling that's where his mind was wandering. The speakers blared with the thumping sounds of Fist Machine. It was their new hit single, "Don't Be Afraid to Sell Yourself Out of Slavery." Frank didn't like the band or the song. Their lyrics were the garbage rock equivalent of Dr. Vo's *Dealing with Yourself.* The band ceaselessly proselytized on the subjects of self-respect and questioning authority. But Fist Machine's pretentiousness didn't affect Frank. The fuzzy guitars and pounding drums filled his head, pushing everything else out. The beat moved his arms, and he managed to clip his finished panels into his portfolio in record time, with factory-like efficiency.

As soon as he finished zipping the binder closed, the phone rang.

Frank saw Steve's number flash across the phone. He picked it up and said, "Hey, Steve. I don't have much time. What's going on?"

"I know, you have that meeting today. I was just calling

to wish you good luck."

"You think I need luck?"

"Come on."

"I'm going there to hand over the package and see if they have any last-minute revisions."

"They paying you the second half of your commission today?"

"No. Don't worry I'll pay you back when I get it."

"I'm not worried about that. You know that. You need me to help you out until they pay up?

"I can charge groceries over the next couple of weeks. I'll be OK."

"You don't want to do that, pay interest on frozen pizzas and soup-in-a-cup. Let me loan you some money for groceries. It's no big deal. Really."

"I don't know."

"Just come by the pharmacy after your meeting. I'll take a late lunch or maybe leave early for the day and we can catch a happy hour at the Mosquito."

"I don't know."

"When's your meeting?"

"Two o'clock."

"How long do you think it will run?"

"An hour tops."

"Just come by the Mosquito at 3:30 or 4 then. I'll just skip lunch and leave early."

"I don't know. I have some errands to run."

"No, you don't. I'll buy you a drink." Steve hung up before Frank could offer any further objections.

Frank considered calling Steve back, but he didn't have much time to argue. Besides, he knew that he would want a drink after the meeting, and it would be nice if he didn't have to pay for it.

Frank tucked his portfolio under his arm and began the search for his car keys.

He arrived at the meeting almost ten minutes late.

The receptionist looked up at Frank as he entered the lobby. She was a summer intern named Sandee. But she seemed older than most college students—and meaner. She took the phone from her ear, almost hung it up, before returning it to her face to say, "Never mind. I'm looking at you right now." She brought the phone down and knocked it around noisily in its cradle.

"Hi, Frank," she said. "Disregard my message. I was just talking to your machine."

"Oh," Frank said. "I didn't realize I was that late." He took a quick glance at his wrist. He had never worn a watch. "What time is it?"

"Almost quarter after."

"I apologize."

"Don't worry about it. Morris has no concept of time either. You can go right in."

Morris' door was ajar, but Frank knocked anyway. The door opened wider with each knock.

Frank saw Morris' thin head poke into view. He was craning his neck, adjusting his spectacles.

"Frank," said Morris. "Is that you?"

"Yes, it is."

"Come in."

A waving hand joined Morris' head. "Come in. I have some people here that I'd like you to meet."

Frank didn't like the sound of that. He was suddenly afraid to push the door open the rest of the way. He stood there and stared at the knob.

Morris cleared his throat. He removed his glasses and squinted with concern. "Would you like something to drink, Frank?"

Frank reached out for the knob and stepped into the room as if both feet had suddenly fallen asleep. His steps belonged to someone else, an old stranger shuffling through a nursing home.

"You know," Frank said, faking a cough. "I could use

some water. If you don't mind."

Morris stood, filled a paper cup at a cooler in the corner of his office, and handed it to Frank.

Frank swallowed extravagantly and pretended to be more than refreshed. "Thank you."

Morris waved at him and returned to his seat. The wave said both 'no problem' and 'quit acting like a jackass.'

Frank found there was only one empty seat in front of Morris' desk. The other two were filled with people he didn't know.

"Frank, I'd like you to meet Jane Courtt," Morris said. "Director of choreography."

Jane raised up half-way out of her chair to shake his hand. Her movements weren't graceful in the least. She was awkward and dumpy. This strange maneuver made it easy to imagine her covering up with a newspaper, rising from the toilet to scold someone who had just invaded her bathroom. She didn't look like a dancer, didn't look like she could ever have been a dancer.

Maybe, this is why she doesn't look happy.

Frank could tell by her firm grip that she was a woman who believed in a strict policy of promptness.

"Good evening." Jane Courtt flashed a smile that said she knew perfectly well it was only mid-afternoon. "It's a pleasure to meet you."

"Likewise," Frank said. "I've heard many good things." Frank had never heard of the woman before.

"And this is Professor Amberhurst. He's the stage director of this fine production."

Professor Amberhurst was a tall thin man and he stood to his full height to greet Frank. He had an awkward manner which suggested that he'd never been wholly comfortable with his lanky bones. His gestures were broad and too careful, the movements of a man learning to walk on stilts. He smiled at Frank from beneath a pointed nose, flashing horse teeth and shimmering gums.

"I've seen your work," Amberhurst said. "Very impressive. Dr. Peel is an old friend. The brochures he showed me were very clean."

"Have a seat, Frank," Morris said. "Show us what you have there."

Frank sat and covered himself with his portfolio. He hugged the thing close to his chest and rested his chin on it. He looked over at Morris like a kid watching from a treetop during a game of hide-and-seek.

Morris reached out his hand, held it there for a long time.

Amberhurst sat down, pulled his left leg up over his right knee, and coughed. Jane Courtt adjusted her clothes, tugged her over-sized sweatshirt, and picked at her drooping stretch pants.

"Frank?" Morris said.

Frank loosened his hold on the portfolio. "I'm open to any suggestions you may have," he said, cautiously pushing the binder away from his body. "We've got plenty of time, right?"

Morris opened and closed his hand. "A couple of weeks. Come on now. Let's have it." He reached out and snatched the portfolio and slapped it on his desk. "I'm sure you have nothing to worry about."

Morris searched the straps, unfastened the buckles, and flipped open the front panel. He scratched his nose on his shirt sleeve and gave Frank a strange look. He adjusted his glasses and flipped through several drawings. He removed his glasses, cleaned them with a soft cloth he kept in his breast pocket, and then put them back on. He flipped to the back of the portfolio and removed his glasses again. He set them on the desk carefully, closed his eyes, and massaged the bridge of his nose.

"What's the matter, Morris?" the professor asked. "Maybe you should get a new prescription."

Morris sighed. The sides of his mouth turned down and

his double chin tripled as he sat back in his chair. He placed both hands on the desktop and pushed off. His chair rolled and its broad leather back smacked against the wall. A fax machine rattled on the top of a nearby credenza.

"What is this?" Morris flipped the portfolio closed with disgust. "Some kind of joke?"

Frank knew he hadn't done the best job for this assignment, but he wasn't expecting this reaction. He'd been sleep-deprived and had taken shortcuts, sure, but it wasn't his worst work. He was pretty confident of that. Then Frank thought that perhaps a panel from an unrelated project had gotten clipped in to the binder on accident. He had procrastinated and compiled the thing in a hurry. Frank suddenly remembered some work he'd recently done for *Cad Fantasy* magazine. Cheesecake drawings danced through his head in thigh-high boots and fishnet stockings.

Frank slouched in his chair and muttered faint apologies under his breath.

"What is it?" Jane asked. She stood and turned the portfolio around to face her. "Oh, my," she said. "Oh. My."

Professor Amberhurst stood at her side and shook his head, clucking his tongue. He flipped through a few drawings and began laughing nervously. He draped his arm over Jane's shoulders as if to console her.

"This is horrible," Jane Courtt said. "Horrible. Unacceptable." She sat down and searched through her purse. "Unacceptable."

Frank stood, peeked around the professor, and expected to see a line-drawing of women in various poll-dancing poses, but he saw mark-up art for the promotional billboard instead. Frank flipped through the rest of the material quickly, in search of the offending panel, and couldn't find it. The portfolio was filled with all the artwork he'd done for the opera house project. Nothing extra had made its way inside. No cabaret. No pin-up nostalgia.

Frank flipped through the binder a second time and was

thoroughly confused. "I'm sorry—"

Jane Courtt interrupted. "You should be. We're good people, Frank."

"I know," Frank said. "I mean, I'm sure you are."

"What's that supposed to mean?" Amberhurst asked, crossing his arms over his chest.

"Nothing," Frank said, raising his hands in surrender. "I'm just confused."

"Give it up, Frank," Morris said.

"I don't understand," Frank said. "I really don't."

"The game is over, buddy," the professor said. "You've had your joke and it was a bad joke anyway."

"Wait a minute," Frank pointed to the binder. "This is exactly what I was paid to produce. I followed the specifications exactly. I just don't understand."

Jane Courtt found her inhaler in a side pocket of her purse and puffed angrily.

"For a minute there," Frank said. "I thought I'd slipped in some drawings from another job. You see, I did this thing for *Cad Fantasy*. I really needed the money."

"Cad Fantasy," said Jane Courtt. "What's that?"

"It's a…Never mind," Amberhurst said.

"You're not making things better for yourself," Morris said.

"Isn't that one of those—?"

"Yes, Jane," Amberhurst said.

"Oh, my."

"Why did you do this, Frank?"

"I can fix whatever it is, I'm sure. Just tell me."

"That's disgusting," Jane Courtt said. "I don't think I like the thought of being in the same room with a pornographer."

"I'm not a pornographer," Frank protested to Jane Courtt's back as she left the room. "They were just drawings."

"Dirty pictures!" Jane Courtt's words echoed from the

hallway.

The receptionist stuck her head in, gave everyone a dirty look, and slammed the door shut.

"She's right," Amberhurst said. "It seems like you could do a bit better than *Cad Fantasy.*"

"This isn't funny," Morris said. "Don't act like everything is OK, Professor. It's not."

"It is funny," Amberhurst said. "Because I don't think this guy has the slightest idea what it is he's done wrong."

"Give me a fucking break." Morris stood up and looked out the window. He put his hands on his hips and dropped his head. "Give me a fucking break. I really don't need this kind of bullshit now, guys. I really don't."

"I'm serious, Morris," Amberhurst said. "The guy doesn't know."

"Know what?" Frank asked. "I'm beginning to think you guys are playing a joke on me."

"Why don't you tell him, Professor?" Morris said. He opened the window and rested his elbows on the ledge. "I don't feel much like playing."

The professor laughed. "You really don't know, do you, Frank?"

"What don't I know?" Frank was starting to get angry.

"Well, for starters," Amberhurst said, "you have no idea what the opera is even about."

Frank couldn't argue with this. He really didn't know.

"If you did, you wouldn't have let the same typographical error appear on every single panel of your presentation."

"What do you mean?"

"The title. You misprinted the title, in every instance."

"It must be the font I used. I can correct that in a matter of minutes."

"It's not the font, Frank," Morris said, slamming the window shut.

Amberhurst stood and looked at the opened binder.

"Nope, it's not the font."

"It has to be," Frank said.

"What is the title, Frank?" Amberhurst asked.

"I know what the title is."

"What is it?"

"*Demon Purse.*"

Amberhurst laughed. His thin legs almost snapped beneath him as he was forced back into his chair.

"What the fuck is wrong with you, Frank?" Morris yelled.

"*Demon Purse!*" The professor cackled. "That would explain the horns."

"This isn't funny," Morris said.

"No, it's not," Frank agreed. He was seriously beginning to believe that he had gotten the title wrong, that he'd put the entire proposal package together and used the wrong title throughout. He'd added horns to the characters to fit an imagined theme, a theme that had absolutely nothing to do with the opera's storyline. And all the while he had no idea that he was doing it. It wasn't a joke. Morris was right. It wasn't funny at all.

"What is the title then?" Frank asked.

"He can't be serious," Morris said.

"You really don't know?" the professor said.

Frank didn't answer.

"*Lemon Purse*," the professor said. "Purse as in pucker. *Lemon Purse* as in 'sour kiss.'"

"What the fuck do you think those little kids are doing on the park bench on the front of the program?" Morris asked. "The girl is carrying a basket of lemons for chrissakes!"

"And she's holding a lemon purse in her lap," the professor said. "Nice little touch of symbolism."

"Demon Purse," Morris said, plopping down in his chair. "Where the fuck did you come up with that?"

"It was an honest mistake," Frank said, unable to believe

what he was saying.

"A stupid mistake," the professor said, "you could have avoided if you'd just taken a trip to the video store."

"I admit it," Frank said. "It was stupid. But I can have it all fixed in under a week. Maybe in a day. I don't think it's that far off. I can use the global replace to change the title, and I can erase the horns without any trouble at all. Just let me look back over the specs again."

"It's too late," Morris said. "I can't complete this project with you. I won't work with someone I can't trust."

"It was a mistake. A stupid mistake."

"It probably isn't my place to say this, Frank," the professor said. "But if you're making mistakes like this, you should really consider seeing a therapist. *Lemon Purse* is probably the most famous opera of the last fifty years. The fact that you aren't at least familiar with the basic storyline is quite unbelievable."

"It's a musical comedy," Frank said, as if this were some kind of defense. "I never liked musical comedies."

"I take offense to that," the professor said, standing to leave. "It's a tragic farce." The professor loped across the room and left the door open behind him.

"I think you should leave now," Morris said.

"I can fix it," Frank pleaded.

"Leave now," Morris said, "And don't follow the professor into the elevator. His nerves are bad."

Frank retrieved his binder from the desk and turned to make his exit.

"Frank?" Morris called after him. "On second thought, just take the stairs."

Chapter 9

Frank met Steve at the Blue Mosquito. The place was empty and dark at five o'clock in the afternoon. Steve sat at the bar with a bottle of beer. The brand matched the advertisement on the coaster. Steve talked to the bartender, face turned up to the television over the bar. The bartender washed glasses. Neither seemed to take much interest in what the other was saying. Politely wasting time together.

Frank took the stool next to Steve, not bothering to announce his presence. He lit a cigarette and feigned interest in the over-muscled men wrestling on the TV.

"Where've you been?" Steve asked.

Frank could feel Steve's head turn, his eyes boring into him. But Frank didn't look away from the choreographed melee flickering overhead. The Mustang Giant was stomping on Buck Lava's chiseled chest. Frank didn't look at Steve when he gave his answer. "Springville Opera House."

"Your meeting lasted nearly three hours?"

Frank ignored the question and turned to get the bartender's attention, careful not to catch Steve's eye. "You guys serve French fries?"

Steve groaned.

The bartender shook his head, twisting a shot glass over his thumb, his hand covered with a stained rag. "We don't serve any food here."

A touch of panic rushed into Steve's voice. "What happened at the meeting?"

"We've got chips," said the bartender, reaching behind the bar. He tossed a heavily worn bag of snack chips on the bar top.

"He won't eat Nacho Crunchies," Steve said. "Will you, Frank? Only French fries."

The bartender shrugged, snatched the chips and tossed them under the bar.

"Only French fries will do," Steve sang in a mocking falsetto.

"Any place near here sell French fries?" Frank asked the bartender.

Steve laughed. "He can't concentrate on anything else when it's decided."

"Yeah," said the bartender. He threw down his rag and glared at Steve and Frank, as if he suspected they were playing a game with him. "You want French fries. We got a Burger Shack right up the block." He jerked his thumb angrily over his shoulder like he was throwing them out.

"Can I come back in here with them?" Frank asked.

The bartender put both hands on the bar. "You gonna buy a drink to go with your beloved French fries?"

"Yeah," Frank said. "So, I can bring them in?"

The bartender rolled his eyes, gave Steve a significant glance, and walked away shaking his head. He threw his rag over his shoulder, pushed through a swinging door, and disappeared into the back of the bar.

"So, are you going to tell me what happened?" Steve asked.

"What's the matter with that guy?" Frank watched the door swing back and forth in its frame.

"Forget it, Frank. He's just like that. Now, tell me what happened?"

"Nothing happened." Frank searched his wallet for French fry money. "I really thought they served food here."

"They never have, for as long as it's been open." Steve swigged his beer and turned his attention back to the television. Buck Lava wept, blood streaming down his face. The Mustang Giant danced around the ring. Steve bared his teeth when he said, "Just go get your god damned French fries."

· · · · · ·

Steve moved to a booth near the back of the bar and waited ten minutes for Frank to return. The windowless door opened and Frank's silhouette appeared against the glaring streetlights. He walked up to the table and dropped a grease-soaked brown paper bag onto the tabletop. He reached into his coat pocket and retrieved a cache of napkins and threw them down next to the bag. He slid into the booth, spread out three layers of napkins, and dumped his fries. He reached the forked fingers of his right hand into the greasy mound and scooped up a mouthful.

"What the hell are you doing?" Steve asked. "That looks like three orders of fries."

"It's four. I'm really hungry." Frank smashed another wad of stringed potatoes and grease into his mouth.

"Are you going to tell me what happened?"

"I asked for three orders. They gave me four."

"At the opera house."

"Like I said. Nothing."

"You wouldn't be drowning yourself in French fries, if nothing happened."

"I lost the job. They want me to return the advance."

"That doesn't sound like nothing."

"It's nothing for me. Less than nothing. I lost money on it."

"They can't expect to get their advance back."

"No?"

"What the hell happened? Weren't you finished with that project?"

"Pretty much."

"Did you say something to offend them?"

"Come on." Frank stuffed his cheeks full with fries. He looked up at the bartender who was now standing next to the table.

"You gonna buy a beer to go with those fries?" the bartender asked, hands on his hips, the stained rag draped over his left shoulder.

Frank didn't answer. He just chewed and looked up at the man with wide, inquisitive eyes.

"Yeah, he'll have a beer," Steve said. "What do you want, Frank?"

Frank swallowed and shook his head.

Steve mouthed the words, *What the fuck is wrong with you?* at Frank, and then offered his apologies to the bartender. "Sorry, buddy. He'll have a Golden Grand. Draught."

The bartender grunted and returned to the bar.

"What the fuck *is* wrong with you?" Steve asked aloud to Frank once the bartender was out of hearing distance.

"I was eating my French fries."

"So?"

"I didn't want to talk with my mouth full." Frank pushed more fries into his mouth. His lips shone with grease. "It's rude."

"You're right, it is. Now, why did they fire you?"

The bartender returned, slammed a full glass down in front of Frank, splashing beer onto his French fry napkin, and walked away.

Frank watched the bartender disappear again into the back room, sopping a couple of fries in spilled beer.

Steve turned away before Frank shoved them into his mouth. "What did you do, Frank?"

"They didn't like the portfolio. We had a misunderstanding."

"What kind of misunderstanding?"

"I misprinted the title on every page."

"Dumb. But. That's an easy fix."

"I put little demon horns all over everything."

Steve laughed. "You're not serious."

Frank turned his attention back to the TV bolted to the

ceiling above the bar. The Harlem Heartbreaker put a platform boot to Jerry "the Hooligan" Mikanowski's forehead. Frank swigged his beer and licked his lips.

"You are serious." Steve sat back in the booth, spreading his palms flat over the table. "Why the hell did you do that?"

"I don't know. It seemed to fit. I thought the opera was called *Demon Purse*."

"You were only a letter off."

"Yep."

"What are you going to do now?"

"I don't know. Look for another gig, I guess."

"You need a little money until you get back on your feet?"

"No. I got a little saved up."

"No, you don't."

Frank picked up another fry and a sliver of wet napkin came with it. He peeled this off with much care and popped the fry into his mouth.

"You're starting to make me sick over here." Steve watched Frank slurp up another fry, it slithered in like a fat yellow worm.

"Can you get me Serapuems?" Frank asked.

"Why? Didn't Vo prescribe some for you?"

"I won't be able to see Vo anymore. I won't be able to pay my CareCo premiums."

"I could help you with that."

"Don't worry about it. I can let it go for a few months."

"You really shouldn't."

"Yeah. Gaps in coverage and all that."

"Right."

"Can you get me some Serapuems?"

"Of course."

"Good." Frank scooped up the last of his French fries. "Delicious."

Chapter 10

Steve returned to work after his midnight lunch break. The neon mortar and pestle blinked overhead as he walked through the sliding glass doors. DrugMart was slow this time of night. He worked just one night shift a month, but it was often enough that his workplace had invaded his dreams. And it was easy now, as he weaved his way to the back of the store, for Steve to see why. The place was eerie after dark. The fluorescent lights buzzed and crackled across shelves of brightly colored merchandise, tightly packed packages of competing bold design. The never-ending music loop, innocuous at noon, now seemed carnivalesque. The patrons moved slower through the aisles, just passing the time, lonely and bored. A waxing machine hummed across the tiles somewhere near the back of the store. Cardboard lay broken and in disarray. Stock boys looked up with looks of wonder, surprise, looks of shame (they were doing a job no one was supposed to see) as Steve walked past them to the pharmacy counter.

There was a short line at the register. Branda, the night pharmacy tech, stapled a receipt to the folded top of a prescription bag, while an old woman struggled with swiping her credit card through the scanner. The man next in line held a box of condoms close to his thigh, trying to conceal the label with his hand and coat sleeve. But the box conspired against him; its cartoonishly phallic blazing sword trademark; the sparkling metallic letters announcing the brand, *Excalibur!*

The man standing at the end of the line held nothing in

his hands. Filthy fingertips hung from the bottoms of frayed coat sleeves. His nails were long and dirty. His overcoat was wrinkled, its front stained with fallen condiments. He stood too close to the condom man. His unshaven face loomed over the man's shoulder.

At first, Steve thought this man was a vagrant. But vagrants usually didn't wait in line. They just wandered the store. He then decided that the man was probably just waiting for his monthly dose of anti-psychotics.

Steve could tell that the man had just walked into the store. The smell of the night's cool wind was swirling around him, along with a deeper, mustier, more personal scent. And the man's photosensitive eyeglasses were now rapidly revealing his eyes.

Frank's eyes.

Steve hadn't seen Frank in over three weeks, not since he'd handed over a bag full of Serapuem samples in a dark corner of the Blue Mosquito. It didn't look like the sleeping pills had brought much sleep or peace of mind to Frank. His lenses now revealed dark circles and hollowed cheeks.

"You have a nice lunch, Steve?" Frank asked. Stained lips cracked as he smiled. "Probably not much open this time of night?"

Steve wanted to say that he'd eaten a huge bag of greasy fries, but managed to control himself. Frank was obviously having a rough time. He looked unstable and serious, incapable of handling snide remarks.

Steve just smiled and nodded his head, distracted himself with the business of finding his keys in the pocket of his lab coat.

He unlocked the pharmacy door, turned the handle, and ducked into the back of the store. He rushed up to Branda and told her to go ahead and take her break. She didn't argue and disappeared into the break room. Steve heard the microwave beep and hum to life. He took the credit card from the old woman's hand and swiped it through the machine, ripped her receipt from the register, and dismissed her with a grunt. He threw the condom man's wrinkled bills in the cash drawer, stuffed his package into a paper sack, folded the receipt over the top, and stapled it shut.

Frank stepped up to the counter and said, "That was rude. Not even a 'hello.'"

"What?" Steve looked over his shoulder into the break room. Branda stirred an instant dinner and placed it back into the microwave for a few dozen more rotations. "Oh, sorry. It wasn't you. It was just that old lady struggling with the card reader. That drives me crazy. It's not that difficult."

"I don't know," Frank said. "I find it kind of tricky."

Steve looked back at Frank and said, "You would."

Frank didn't smile. He looked down and searched through his coat pockets. He piled an array of gum wrappers, dirty facial tissues, and wrinkled receipts on the counter top. "Don't worry about it," he said, and removed a tattered pack of cigarettes and put one in his mouth.

"You know you can't smoke in here." Steve looked toward the front of the store to make sure no employees were walking his way.

"I know. I'm just getting ready. I can't stay long. I have to get up early tomorrow."

"No, you don't."

Frank shrugged his shoulders and scooped the trash from the counter top and stuffed his pockets. "So, how are things, Steve?" Frank didn't look up from the business of filling up his coat. "I haven't seen you in awhile. How's Jill?"

Steve shook his head and walked back out through the door and met Frank on the other side of the counter. "Jill's fine. I'm fine." He sighed. "You look like shit."

Frank didn't respond.

"Come on." Steve stepped into an aisle filled with topical creams and powders, gesturing for Frank to follow. "Let's step over here and talk. I'll be able to see someone if they come up to the counter."

Frank followed, and they stood facing a wall of Vulvacor and Labial, talking to each other from the sides of their mouths.

"I'm going to be sleeping here in an hour or so," Frank said. "I took three Serapuems on the drive over."

"Three?"

"Four. I've developed quite a tolerance."

Steve lowered his voice. "Well, I can't get you any more until the end of the month. The distributors only drop off so many samples. And, technically, they're not even supposed to be giving me samples."

"That's not why I'm here." Frank placed a bag of cold sore tabs back on its hook, pulled a row of fungal cream forward to the edge of a shelf.

"What are you doing?"

"Fronting the shelves."

"Why?"

Frank straightened an assortment of fragranced enema kits. "I was wondering if you could get me some Vril patches."

"Vril patches?"

"Keep your voice down. It's embarrassing enough as it is."

"I didn't know you had a girlfriend." *He couldn't have a girlfriend, the way he looks right now.*

"I don't."

"Then why?"

"You know the answer to that. I shouldn't have to come out and say it."

"Hey, I'm sorry. I never really thought of it like that."

"Can you get me a box?"

"I guess."

"Tonight?"

"I don't know."

Frank slipped a tube of a water-based lubricant in his pocket and looked up threateningly at Steve. "Tonight?" he asked again, raising an eyebrow.

"Put that back, and I'll see what I can do."

Frank placed the tube neatly back on the shelf and Steve disappeared behind the pharmacy door.

He returned with a paper bag stapled shut with a bogus receipt.

"How many do I get?"

"Is thirty enough?"

"Well—"

"I don't want to hear about it. Just go." Steve pointed to the front of the store.

Frank took the sack. Steve waved away his 'thank yous' and ushered him down the aisle.

Steve waited until Frank was just beyond the giant brick wall of cased Killer Cola, and then called after him, "Hey, take care of yourself. OK?" Steve's voice revealed more guilt than he would have liked, and he tried to cover up with another good-bye, which came off sounding more sarcastic than he'd intended. "Give me a call. You know, when you're not too busy."

Frank didn't turn around, didn't wave.

Steve returned to the counter and found two people waiting for their prescriptions. He rang them up and took their money without looking at them. His mind was still following Frank down the aisle. His dark crumpled form had been in such sharp contrast to his surroundings, like a sewer rat crawling over a white lace tablecloth.

It's amazing how far someone could fall in just a few weeks. Steve sprayed the counter top and wiped it clean. He couldn't help but wonder what it would take to break him, to bring him down to where Frank was right now.

Then the phone rang, startling him. They didn't get many calls this late at night. He looked up at the phone and saw that the blinking light indicated an inside line. Someone was calling from register three at the front of the store. He picked up the phone. It was Selma Rae. Her deep, scratchy voice was unmistakable.

"Hey, hey," she said. "Do I got Steve on the phone?"

"How are you doing, Selma?"

"Good, good."

"What can I do for you?"

"Your buddy just left here. He just walked out the door. You could probably catch him if you wanted to."

"I saw him."

"Oh," said Selma, distracted. "That will be fourteen dollars even."

"You're talking about Frank, right?"

"Yeah. I just saw him."

"Frank's my brother."

"Right. Have a good night, honey."

"OK, Selma. Good night."

"I wasn't talking to you."

"Sorry."

"You want to hear something funny?"

"I don't know."

"It's about your buddy."

"Brother."

"Right. He just walked out of here with a cigarette dangling from his mouth."

"Sorry about that."

"Don't be sorry. He wasn't smoking it or anything. It's just that it seems strange, considering he bought a box of nicotine patches on his way out. Maybe it was his last smoke, huh?"

"You're kidding?"

"Nope. People do some damn funny things."

"Yes, they do, Selma. Have good a night."

Steve hung up the phone, confused and worried. He didn't think for a moment that Frank was planning to quit smoking, and it was dangerous to smoke while wearing the patch. And he had no idea what could happen if someone wore the nicotine patch while wearing the Vril patch. It certainly couldn't be good for the heart. He'd have to look it up.

Steve finished out his shift and stopped by the front counter on his way out to the parking lot. He picked up a package of nicotine patches, sliced open the plastic with a fingernail, and removed the disclosure packet within. He scanned the pages until he found a consumer advisory that read: *If you have vivid dreams, you may wish to remove this patch at bedtime.*

Chapter 11

Steve folded the newspaper clipping into squares, stuffed it into his shirt pocket, and climbed out of his car. He walked up the gravel path to Frank's front porch and stood in a pile of newspapers still wrapped in plastic. He knocked on the screen door, waited, and then opened it to bang the knocker on the wooden door beyond. There was no answer. He tried the knob and found it unlocked. He turned it and opened the door, pushed his face through. The smell that met him was strong with sweat socks and the ghosts of greasy meals.

"Frank? Are you here?" said Steve as he pushed his way inside. He left the door open to allow some fresh air in.

The front room seemed oddly spare, but messy at the same time. The floor crawled with twisted socks, fast food bags, Chinese take-out cartons, beer and cola cans, and instant dinner tins.

Then Steve noticed a place by the stairs where the carpet was flattened and brighter than that in the rest of the room. An errant coaxial cable curled from the wall. Frank's television set was missing. Steve thought that Frank had been robbed. But then he noticed another clean spot in the carpet, a larger one, where Frank's beloved recliner once rested.

No, he's just done some rearranging of his furniture. He's probably just hauled everything he needs upstairs to make it easier for him to avoid visitors when they come to the door. Frank had done things like this before. When his last girlfriend left him, he had installed all black window treatments and low wattage bulbs.

Frank was probably sitting upstairs, drunk out of his mind, in front of the television set, feeling sorry for himself.

Steve started up the stairs, intent on slapping the man out of his self-pity, when a strange noise stopped him on the second step. It was a low whimpering noise, a cross between a frightened puppy and a muzzled monkey. Thoughts of robbery returned to Steve, and he pictured Frank locked in a closet upstairs, bound and gagged, duct tape wrapped around his skull.

Steve continued up the stairs with more caution, listening closely for footsteps, but all he heard was the whimpering sound growing more frenzied, more rhythmic.

The hall was dark at the top of the stairs. There were three doors. Two led to bedrooms, one led to the bathroom. All were left wide open. The last door on the right was Frank's room, and a flickering light escaped the doorway into the hall.

Frank's missing television set.

Steve approached the doorway and peered in. The room was too small for all the furniture now squeezed inside. The recliner was crammed between a dresser and the bed, so that Frank would have to crawl over his mattress in order to get to the door. The big screen TV rested on a second dresser too small to hold it. The TV almost completely covered an eastward window, blotting out the sun. When Steve saw what was displayed on its screen he almost turned around and left.

A woman's face filled the set's frame. Mascara poured down her cheeks. Smeared lipstick made her lips appear swollen and bruised. Her top row of teeth clamped down on her lower lip with intense concentration. Her eyes were closed. She whimpered as she was pushed forward toward the camera by the mechanical thrusts of a man positioned off-camera behind her.

The focus of the scene changed. Steve turned away, but not before catching a glimpse of a man's sweaty face, the gross detail captured in a way that only cheap video equipment can achieve. The man's skin was blotchy and scarred. His pores were large and dark. His mustached upper lip was turned up in a snarl to reveal yellow, crooked teeth. His eyes were half closed and his chin nodded with the rhythm of his thrusting torso.

Steve tried not to look back at the screen. His eyes combed the floor as the mustached man's growls filled the room. Steve found a stack of rented DVD cases next to Frank's recliner, along with a mangled box of Vril samples. Foil wrappers from both Vril and Nicotine transdermal patches littered the floor.

Steve sat down on the bed, peered around the back of the recliner, and found Frank asleep in his chair. His eyelids were flickering. A string of drool wound down through his unkempt beard and onto his naked chest. Frank's torso and arms were covered with plots of dried glue, where old transdermal patches had been torn away.

Steve noted two fresh patches, one Vril, one Nicotine, pasted just under Frank's right collarbone. The patches were transparent and Steve could see Frank's skin raised and red beneath them. Then he noticed that Frank was naked from the waist down.

Frank's erection looked worn, almost dark purple in this light. And it twisted up to the left. This glistening, misshapen thing reminded Steve of a gnarled yarrow root.

Steve looked back to the TV screen, at the woman's smeared face. Her hair stuck to her forehead and her eyes focused intently, threateningly, on the camera. Her mouth hung open, revealing a shimmering pink tongue.

Steve reached into his shirt pocket, touched the newspaper clipping, and considered just leaving it on Frank's bed for him to find when he finally woke up. But then another idea came to mind. He thought it might do Frank some good for him to know that someone else knew what he'd been up to these past few weeks. Maybe he could be shamed into getting his life back together again.

Steve left Frank, went to the kitchen, retrieved a glass of cold water, and returned to the bedroom. He held the glass over Frank and smiled, thinking back to his college days when a prank like this would have seemed hilarious. Now it just seemed strange and sad. He was filled with a feeling like remorse, a heaviness invaded his limbs, as he stood there looming over his brother with an empty prankster's grin spread across his face.

This ought to cool him down and wake him up.

Steve dumped the glass into Frank's lap. And found himself jumping back, almost falling backwards over the corner of the bed, when he saw that the cold water had exactly the opposite effect.

Frank came.

And when Steve regained his balance, he found the TV screen filled with a close-up of a man ejaculating toward the camera. He flinched when he heard someone off-camera, possibly the director, shout, "All right, there's our money sh—" And laughed when the voice was cut-off way too late through sloppy editing.

Frank somehow had fallen into a deeper sleep. His eyelids no longer moved. He was still erect, despite the cold water, and the fresh climax dribbling over his bare flesh onto the recliner's cushion.

The scene on the TV changed to the interior of an executive's "office," which was really just the same hotel room with the furniture rearranged. The writing desk was pulled away from the wall and two chairs were positioned in front of it. The room wasn't large enough for the cameraman to avoid getting the corner of the queen-size bed in the frame. A fat executive in a rumbled suit was dictating to his secretary, who wore a mini-skirt, suit jacket, and tie. They spoke to each other in flat tones, barely audible under the too-loud soundtrack of drum machine and wah-wah guitar.

Steve turned off the TV and shook his head at his brother. He was now determined to wake him and instill a rehabilitating sense of shame in the man. He reached over, pinched his cheek and twisted it until Frank's eyes popped open.

"Holy shit," Frank said, in a tone that matched exactly the flat delivery of the actors in the films he'd been watching. The Serapuems were still thick in his blood. "Steve?"

Steve twisted Frank's cheek even harder. "Frank, wake up, Frank."

"I'm awake. Let go of my fucking face."

Steve let go, smiled down on his brother, and waited.

Frank's eyelids drooped, almost closed again, and tears welled in their corners. He reached up and rubbed his sore cheek, wiped his nose on his forearm, and looked thoroughly confused. "What the hell's going on?"

"You tell me."

Frank looked down and saw his exposed genitals. He groaned and pulled himself out of his chair with great effort. He bent over, presented his spread ass cheeks, and rummaged through a pile of laundry, wiped himself off with a dirty towel, and pulled on a pair of stained boxer shorts. He turned back around, glared at Steve, and sopped up the seat of his recliner with the towel. He spotted his remote control at the back of the chair, retrieved it, and slid it under his nose, sniffing with a disgusted look on his face. He flopped back into the chair, arms crossed over his chest, tapping a button on the remote on his way down.

The TV screen flashed on. The executive and his secretary were atop the desk now. Their movements were exaggerated and wild, fools joined in a slapstick pantomime rodeo.

"Turn that off," Steve said.

"You're right. It's not working anymore."

"What do you mean?"

"I can't blot it out with this anymore," Frank jabbed the

remote at the set and an image of an open-handed slap to the secretary's posterior faded slowly away into blank screen. "It worked for a while. I was able to force myself to dream other dreams."

"Other dreams?"

Frank turned away from the blank screen, turned his glassy eyes on Steve. "I told you about the doll's arm. The crack in your living room."

Steve scratched behind his ear. "You're talking about the dream you saw Vo about?" He reached down and picked up a DVD case and read its title. *Head Nurse 3*. "You've been having it again?"

"I had that same dream every single night since my first visit with Dr. Vo."

Steve picked up another video. *Eat it While It's Hot.* He tapped it against his knee, threw it to the floor, and picked up another. *Hardly Working.* "You never told me that."

"It doesn't matter," Frank said, twirling the remote in his left hand, staring into the darkened television.

"You can go see him again, you know."

"My coverage ran out two months ago."

"No shit. I was offering to pay for it, asshole."

Frank threw the remote. It rattled behind the dresser. The battery panel snapped off and landed on the bed next to Steve.

"I don't need to see Vo. I can take care of this myself."

"How exactly have you been taking care of it?"

Frank looked at him with half-closed lids, smiled from the left side of his mouth. "I forced out an incubus by invoking the succubi."

Steve looked into Frank's eyes, searching deep for the clue, the twitch that would tell him that his brother was joking, putting him on. But Frank was serious, and seriously frightened.

"I decided that I'd rather have my soul stolen by a demoness," Frank said.

"Who wouldn't."

"I slap on a Vril and a Nicotine patch about four hours before I plan to go to bed. I've been watching these things to get in the mood." He picked up an empty DVD case and read the title, *Chastity's Revenge*. I fast-forwarded through most of this one. I guess I do with most of them. When I've seen enough of Chastity or Esther, or whoever, I take two Serapuems, and I'm actually with them. I've been with Chastity here a dozen times. Her and Kimba Lakes at the same time."

"In dreams?"

"Some of the best dreams I ever had. Sleeping on Nicotine makes them real."

"No. You just have less restful sleep. When you have less restful sleep, you have a tendency to remember more about your dreams."

"Fine, have it your way." Frank grimaced as he pinched the Vril patch from his skin. "All I know is that I've been through some pretty strange bedrooms lately. It was fun at first." He peeled off the Nicotine patch. "But, like I said, the incubus came back. The succubi just weren't strong enough."

"What is this incubus shit?"

"That's what I call the doll's arm."

"What's so scary about a fucking doll's arm?"

"It persists. Every night it made its appearance, and then the succubi came and blotted it out for a while. But now it's back. Not every night. But I know it will be. It's just a matter of time."

"Listen, Frank." Steve removed the folded newspaper clipping from his pocket. "I brought something for you."

Frank turned his attention to the glue splotches on his chest. He began picking at them, pouting. "I'll be getting a head job and I'll look down and see Harley Cheeks deep-throating the damn thing."

"The doll arm?"

"Yeah, the fucking arm. One night, Becky Highborn and Bambi Biggs burst through my back door with chainsaws, wearing strap-ons."

Steve laughed. "Terrifying."

"They tried to rape me."

Steve didn't stop laughing.

"They were baby-doll arm strap-ons, Steve."

"For some reason, that doesn't make it seem any less humorous."

"Give me a break."

Steve looked down at the newspaper clipping, handed it to Frank. "Here."

"What's this?"

"It's a break. It's a job."

Frank unfolded the clipping. "It's a classified ad."

"It's a job, Frank."

Frank read through the ad. "I don't know if I want to spend my days drawing hammers."

"Drawing toothpicks would be better than what you've been doing."

"Yeah, I need to shave." Frank folded the clipping into a little square. "Clean up the place a bit. I really need to go to the library."

"Do you want the job?"

"I do need a job. I mean, I'll apply for it."

"Would you do it?"

"If they hired me. Sure, I'd draw power tools for a little while."

"Good. That's what you'll be doing. You have an interview on Monday."

"What are you talking about?"

Steve slapped Frank on the knee and winked. "Don't worry, it's just a formality. You already got the job." He stood and scanned the bedroom with gloating eyes. "But you still might want to shower, clean yourself up a bit, before you go."

Chapter 12

Read this sentence. Now, look away from this book.
Stop!
Look all around you—really take it all in—*before going on to the next sentence. We really mean it.*

Frank read this passage twice, looked up at the bookshelves surrounding his reading nook in the local public library, and then returned to the pages of *Control Your Dreams!: A Field Guide for Lucid Dreamers*.

Now that you've looked away, re-read the five sentences above. Are they the same sentences you read just a second ago? If the answer is yes, you're awake. If the answer is no, you're dreaming. This very simple test is the first step in mastering the art of lucid dreaming. Make this little 'reality test' a habit in your daily life. It will soon become second nature, and you'll find yourself doing it in your dreams. No book, no label, no street sign, will read the same way twice in a dream. Knowing this, recognizing this—realizing that you're dreaming while *you're dreaming!— is the key to controlling your dreams.*

Frank closed the book, read its front cover, looked away, and then read it again. The title hadn't changed. He placed the book on a stack of ten other dream reference books and headed up to the checkout counter.

Chapter 13

The wheels of three overflowing shopping carts rattled across the blacktop at the Old Grocer. A stock boy named Cliff followed a bagger named Charley, who followed a customer in a ragged overcoat. They traveled single file, pushing their carts toward a rusted-out vehicle. The car was in such an advanced state of disrepair that its make and model were no longer distinguishable.

Cliff had never seen anything like it in his entire career at the Old Grocer. Although, he'd only worked there a year, he'd never been asked to follow a customer around the store while he filled up three cartloads of cans and dried goods. He'd never seen a customer, whose appearance and smell seemed to indicate that he was homeless, spend so much money on groceries.

Cliff stopped behind the man's car and waited while he fumbled for his keys. He searched each coat pocket twice before searching his pants. He finally found them in the back pocket of his jeans and seemed quite surprised to find them there. Cliff figured the guy did his paint job about seventy-five dollars' worth of damage with those keys as he searched for the lock. The trunk was empty except for a worn golf bag and a few straggling clubs.

Cliff turned to Charley, poked him in the arm, and gave him a dirty look for staring. Charley was his cousin, and he'd been staring at people all his life. He nodded at him to begin helping the poor bum load his groceries into the trunk. Cliff stepped up after him, and soon the trunk was filled with overflowing bags, toilet paper bundles, and cases of beer and soda. Cliff noticed the strange customer taking sharp double-takes at any item which escaped the flimsy plastic bags, like he was taking a mental note for later, so that if he found anything missing he could place the blame on these boys.

No. Cliff didn't like this guy. This customer. The man's beard was speckled with food. His clothes were crumpled. His fingers were stained with smoke, his hair styled with ancient scalp oils. Cliff found himself disliking filthy people in general the longer he stood there. And Cliff had a tendency to lose his manners with those he didn't like. He reached over and opened the car door without asking permission and began hastily shoveling the bagged goods into the back seat.

"You in some kind of hurry, kid?" the customer asked.

Cliff stopped and looked at the bum, not answering, waiting to be given the OK to resume filling up the man's car with Apple Crisps, Handiwipes, and cans of NoodleZoni.

"What's your name, son?" The man squinted to read Cliff's name tag. He turned away, then sharply back again, and reread the badge. "Cliff?"

Cliff didn't answer.

"Nice to meet you, Cliff," the bum said. "I'm Frank."

Cliff stared, taking in the man's smell, and let his disgust feed his growing hatred.

"Now, Cliff," Frank said. "You're not a valet and I'm not a woman." He looked at Charley, read his name tag twice, and asked, "Charley, I don't look like a woman?"

"Not at all," said Charley.

Cliff snorted. *You don't even look human. I could choke you out, right now.*

"How old are you, Charley?" Frank said. He was still smiling at Cliff.

"Fifteen,"

"You have a car?"

"I get my license next week,"

Frank winked at Cliff, turned to Charley, looked at his

name tag twice, and said, "That's not what I asked you. Charley."

Charley was staring. He caught himself, and turned his head. "I'm saving up."

"How much you got saved?"

Charley shuffled his feet. "About three hundred."

Cliff couldn't help but laugh. "Jeez, Charley. You'll get your first car just in time to drive yourself to college."

"Do you have a bike?" Frank asked, ignoring Cliff.

Charley turned red and bit his lower lip.

"Yeah, he's got a bike," Cliff said, "with a basket on it."

"Really?" Frank said. "I like baskets. Is it attached to the handlebars, or to the back of the seat?"

Charley straightened up to defend himself. "To the back of the seat," he said proudly.

"That's certainly much less girly," Cliff said.

"Hey, it's functional. I don't like backpacks," Charley said.

"It's got tassels hanging from the handlebars, too," Cliff said.

"No, it doesn't."

"Pink and yellow."

"Shut up, Cliff."

"Yes, be quiet," Frank said. "Me and Charley are talking business here."

Don't you tell me to be quiet! Cliff wanted to say something, but he just stood there, not believing that he'd let this human filth tell him to be quiet. He struggled with this for a while, paralyzed with indecision, but finally he had to admit that this man scared him. The bum's eyes shone from beneath the filth, a reflection of a deep and dangerous inner world. His eyes projected this torment and sadness outward, covering everything, imbuing the outer world with false proofs and confirmations for his madness.

This guy is seeing things right now, things Charley and me can't.

"I want to make a deal with you, Charley," Frank said,

wiping his nose on his coat sleeve. "I sell you my car for your three hundred."

"Really?" Charley said, excited. Then he looked at the car's rusted body and sagging tires. "I don't know."

"You'll have to throw in your bike, too."

"You don't want this piece of shit," Cliff said.

"The engine's fine," Frank said. "It will run for awhile."

"I might think about it." Charley walked around to the other side of the car and counted bumps and scars, scratches and rusted holes. "I have to give you my bike?"

"What are you going to do with it?" Frank patted the car. "You'll be driving this baby."

Cliff laughed. "And what exactly is it?" he asked. "Come on, Charley. You can't even tell what kind of car it is."

"I don't care what it looks like," Charley said. "As long as it runs."

"It runs," Frank said. "Are you interested?"

"I might be." Charley ran his hand over the hood and then brushed off the dirt onto his jeans. "Three hundred isn't bad."

"No, it's not." Frank reached into his coat pocket. He removed a stack of business cards bound in a lint-covered rubberband. "Here's my card, kid. It's got my address and phone number on it. You give me a call, ride your bike over, and I'll sign over the title. You can drive away with it tonight, if you want."

Business card? Cliff couldn't believe what he was seeing. *What the hell kind of business can this guy be in?*

Charley was obviously thinking the same thing, he was studying the card closely, his face twisted up with confusion. "You're a graphic designer?" he asked.

"Oh, yeah, the best in town," Frank said, with just a hint of sarcasm. He read and reread the top card in his stack before stuffing them back into his pocket. "So, do we have a deal, Charley?"

"Probably. I'll think about it." Charley read the address

from the card. "Weirmont. That's not too far from Wild Oaks, is it?"

"Nope."

"That's not too far to ride. I think I might do it."

"Good," Frank said. "Just give me a call."

Charley nodded his head and walked away, the groceries forgotten. He clutched the business card as if it were a winning lottery ticket, and made his way up the parking lot and through the sliding electric doors of the Old Grocer.

"Where the hell is he going?" Cliff asked.

"Guess it's just me and you, buddy," Frank said.

"Yeah, I guess so." Cliff looked after his cousin. He picked up two bags filled with sugary cereal and sandwich cookies and threw them in the back seat of the car, not caring as their contents scattered onto the floor mats.

"Be careful, kid," Frank said.

Cliff ignored him. He knew he wasn't getting a tip.

Chapter 14

Frank, dressed in black, mounted his new bike, which he'd spray-painted black for the express purpose of making stealthy night missions. He turned around and patted the duffel bag of supplies in the basket behind his seat, making sure that he hadn't forgotten it, and then pedaled off down his dark suburban street, avoiding the bright circles thrown by the street lights.

Frank had spent the last two months sleeping, dreaming, and facing his recurring nightmare head on. He'd now spent countless lucid hours at Steve's party, investigating, interviewing the party-goers, searching the back rooms for any clue to the truth of his dream. The more he lived in this dream, the more control he was able to exercise over it. Details changed with his will. He stayed longer each night, laughing and dancing, or sneaking off to look for hidden panels in the garage, depending on his mood. He'd taken guests to the back bedrooms on more than one occasion.

The dream had stopped frightening him after he'd learned how to recognize that he was dreaming. It hadn't taken him long to overcome his fear of the magician. It only took him a week of lucid dreams before he was able to stay in the dream past the piercing trick. And he found that he came out unscathed. The magician simply removed the pipes and the wounds disappeared. He even held the magician's hand one evening and they bowed together as if they both had worked in tandem to produce this amazing feat. Frank had even spent long nights talking to the magician, one-on-one. Frank, knowing he was dreaming, asked probing questions, but the magician, provided predictably nonsensical answers.

It was this persistent illogic of dreams that frustrated Frank. No matter how cognizant he was in the dream world, its fluid fantasies still confounded him. Being aware of the dream, able to see it clearly, didn't allow him to make sense of any of its strangeness. It only made the bizarre more vivid, the twisted more deeply felt.

Finally, he decided that the answers to his dream didn't lie in the dream world at all, that the dream had been telling him all along exactly where the answers were to be found: Steve's house. In Steve's living room.

Something had happened there, or something would. A secret was hidden in the walls. And Frank was headed there now to find out exactly what. His duffel bag was full with his makeshift burglary kit, amongst other things. He would have to sneak inside. He couldn't possibly ask for permission to investigate, because Jill and Steve would never grant their permission. Frank was certain that whatever was hidden there, they didn't want him to see.

Frank stopped in front of a familiar house to catch his breath. He'd been pedaling wildly for some time and hadn't even noticed. His mind had been too busy searching Steve's living room. But now he was starkly aware of his surroundings. He knew exactly where he was. He'd stopped in front of the house which belonged to the faceless girl from his dream. Frank didn't know who it really belonged to. But as he stared at it now, he made a mental note to find out.

Frank watched the darkened front windows of the house, almost hoping a featureless face would reveal itself from behind a curtain. But he lost his courage in the end and quickly pedaled away when an upstairs light flipped on.

He rode slowly the rest of the way to Steve's, avoiding street lights, careful not to show himself or make a sound. He stopped in front of a dark row of bushes across from Steve's driveway and listened. The front of the house was lit by a single bulb over the front porch. None of the windows were illuminated. Frank knew they wouldn't be. He knew that Steve and Jill went to bed early. They slept soundly and awoke well-rested every morning. It was something they bragged about. Yes. Steve and Jill would be first to say that they are both happy and healthy people.

Frank dismounted and walked his bike up the driveway, around the back of the house, and leaned it against the steps leading up to Jill's prized screened-in porch. It was her masterpiece of wicker and hanging plants.

Frank crouched by the basement window and peered through at a computer table and swivel chair. They seemed abandoned and useless in shadow. Frank imagined two robots, powered down for the night, retired to their storage cabinet, heads bowed in the darkness. He opened his duffel bag very slowly so that the zipper made no audible zip. He reached inside, retrieved a screwdriver and a hammer and wondered exactly what he intended to do with them. He studied the window and discovered that it was unlocked. He wedged the screwdriver under the bottom panel and pried it open. Frank then tucked away his tools and slid down into the basement, snatching his bag down after him as soon as his feet were firmly planted on the water-resistant carpeting.

Frank held the bag close to his chest as he climbed the basement steps. He opened the door onto a quiet kitchen, dark except for a light flickering over the range. The kitchen was the middle of the house. Steve and Jill's master bedroom was located down the hall to his right. He squinted through the darkness and found their bedroom door firmly shut and no light spilling out from beneath it. Then Frank stepped softly over the plush carpet to the darkened party room on the opposite side of the house. The room smelled of stale smoke, air freshener sprayed over spilt beer. Moonlight poured through the windows leading out to Jill's porch, filtering through plants, throwing jagged shadows on the walls. The television set was a black, hulking box, a darker, brooding robot cousin to the chair and computer desk residing in the basement. The mouth of the fireplace was a tunnel leading to a lair of evil dwarfs. The glass covering the erotic art pieces glared, their silver frames shined.

Frank lowered his duffel bag onto the couch and walked slowly across the living room and touched the wall between two pictures. It was perfect, clean, cool against his fingertips. He pressed fingers into it, and it was solid. It hadn't been recently repaired to conceal a crack. He turned his back to the wall and took a quick look around the room. Nobody was there. He sensed nothing out of the ordinary.

He took a seat next to his duffel bag to think. Maybe if he sat in this room for a while, just sat there letting its presence wash over him, something would come to him, something might be understood. He unzipped his bag again and removed a can of NoodleZoni and a can opener. He twisted the lid off and reached inside his bag. His hand came out with a spoon and he spent the next ten minutes leisurely eating his cold noodles in spicy tomato sauce, staring at the wall, ready for it to open its mouth and taunt him with its silver-gray tongue. He scraped the last few noodles from the bottom of the can. He pushed himself from the couch in four separate motions in an effort not to rattle his bag of tools. He returned to the wall of erotic art and scratched with his over-long fingernails. He couldn't remember the last time he'd tended to them. Their tips were almost blackened now, shiny and jagged. The paint came away easily as he chipped and scratched. Flakes fell to the carpet and the vibrations, the friction of this activity, gave him the jitters. But Frank continued. He'd suddenly decided there was something hidden there. He persisted until he'd removed a ragged patch in the paint. Dull plaster shown through. He pressed his fingers through the plaster with ease and the wall broke away, leaving a hole exactly the same shape and size as the crack in his dream, and the emptiness beyond was just as stark, just as deep. Frank felt the same sense of vertigo he felt in his dreams as he peered into the hole, a feeling like leaning over a bottomless chasm, teetering on the brink with only the flimsiness of a single coat of dried paint between him and endless free fall.

Frank took a step back. He stared at the crack in the wall, barely able to believe it was real. He wondered if his brother knew, and quickly decided that he didn't, he couldn't. Steve had never been able to keep a secret. But Jill on the other hand...

Frank bent over and peered through the crack again. He saw a faint shimmer in the blackness. About three feet in, but it was impossible to tell for certain. The hole could be a foot deep or could go on forever. Frank retrieved a screwdriver from his duffel bag, twirled it through his fingers, and thrust its pointed end into the wall with a vicious stab.

A triangle of plaster chipped off and tumbled into the darkness. It was preternaturally bright. Frank watched the simple flashing triangle tumble, twinkling, becoming smaller and smaller, as it fell into the void.

He brought the screwdriver down again. And again.

Two more cracked triangles winked out of existence.

A slick silver wash of light swam up from the depths a moment after the triangles disappeared. It grew larger and more solid as it neared the crack in the wall. The baby doll arm's metallic gray flesh rotated in the darkness, a thing of magic, reflecting its own phantom light. Its chubby, cupped hand stopped a few inches from Frank's nose and remained perfectly still. He blinked and the arm spun in a hundred directions at once, but became still again as soon as Frank regained his focus on the piece of plastic he'd come to call the incubus.

"What are you doing here?" Frank whispered at the detached baby-doll's arm.

The broken toy didn't speak. It struck out at Frank, lashed him on the forehead, instantly drawing blood.

Frank leapt back from the hole, fell onto the couch, rattling his bag of burglary tools. Then he crawled to the floor and kept perfectly still, belly and palms pressed firmly to the carpet, as if he were preparing to do a push-up. He listened for footsteps, tired voices. He stared at the hole in the wall as he listened. The gray baby doll arm twisted and twirled, making its way around the edge of the hole. It taunted him, compelled him.

Frank crawled across the carpet, dragging his pelvis and legs like a maimed lizard. He then found himself laying his palms on the wall in a manner that he found worshipful and disturbing. He climbed to one knee and attempted to peek through the wall once again. But the doll hand swatted him away, digging out a swatch of Frank's hair from the scalp.

He tumbled back and knocked into a flimsy floor lamp that had suddenly grown in the center of the room. Frank looked up at its lampshade that shook near the ceiling, blaring, rocking back and forth, ringing like an ancient church's bell. It cast a sort of sick truth over the bleak furniture. The couch blurred into a huddled mass of nude figures, uncomfortably intertwined to mimic the shape of a couch in darkness. They wore masks, but their faces betrayed a type of concentration and strain which contradicted their erotic arrangements.

The bobbling lamp continued to sway, revealing easy chairs comprised of two pairs of writhing couples. The television became an aquarium filled with a perfect cube of flesh.

Frank struggled to stop the lamp from moving. It fought him, bucked him several times before growing tired. Frank brought it down and snapped off the light. And then he found two wing nuts at the base of the lamp's head and twisted them off. He suddenly realized that he'd disassembled this type of floor lamp before. He wasn't sure where. But he found himself unsnapping its parts and concentrically snapping it back together again in one neat compact package. When Frank was finished, the lamp was reduced to the size of an easy-to-use handheld flashlight. And it was turned off, extinguished. That was the most important thing. Frank imagined what it would have looked like from the street, the windows suddenly ablaze with the crazed flashlight beams of a mad dancing burglar.

He held tight to the contracted floor lamp for a few minutes and waited, listened.

A dog barked in the distance.

Crickets carried on, chirping undisturbed. No footsteps, no raised, groggy voices.

Frank returned to the crack in the wall. The doll's arm was gone. He reached both hands into the crack and hoisted himself up. He looked into the hole and saw the silvery wave return, joined by a dozen glowing eyes. The eyes blinked and reproduced. A dozen more eyes came into being with every blink.

Frank saw the night sky. The eyes were stars stabbing through fog, worms of light sprouting up through thick purple mud. Frank was looking through a hole that looked onto Steve's backyard. A line of trees separated Steve's property from his neighbor's. Frank narrowed his eyes at the tree rooted directly across from the crack in the wall and found an identical crack in the tree's bark. He pressed his face deeper into the hole to get a better look. His nose and his eyes bulged through the other side of the wall. And the doll's arm returned, poking out of the tree, waving an excited parade wave.

Frank tore himself from the wall, feeling as if he were really onto something. He soft-stepped it down the basement stairs as stealthily and as quickly as he could. He slithered out of the cracked basement window and onto the cement back patio with a grace and ease for which he felt oddly proud. He made his way around to the side of the house without disturbing too many leaves. Only a few twigs cracked under his weight. When he reached the living room's outside wall, it didn't take him long to find the tree he'd spotted from inside. He marched over to it, crushing dried leaves and not caring; the master bedroom was on the opposite side of the house.

The doll's arm twirled as he approached. A soft jewelry box tune played as it turned. Frank grabbed for the arm, but it was much too fast, disappearing inside the tree long before his fingers came within reach.

Frank hugged the tree. He smashed his face against the tree's bark and looked inside. He found nothing there at first, and then the silver wave. The eyes and then the stars. The universe opened for Frank, put on a private show inside that tree. Frank felt like a five year-old stuck to an ancient nickelodeon's eyepiece. He was scared, but thrilled with the night inside the tree. And the stars. He couldn't think of anything more beautiful.

And the hole in this wonderful tree revealed another tree filled with stars. And the next tree revealed another. A trail of scarred trees wound through the neighborhood, tying it together, a trail of lost worlds. Clusters of star systems tunneled through a planned forest of perennials and pine.

The tiny silver-gray arm waved him forward, poked out and danced, from the hole in every tree, until Frank was just a few feet away, and then would disappear inside the trunk. Frank followed the arm through a maze of manicured lawns, to a line of trees bordering a brick house poured from the same mold as Steve's.

He peered into a tree in the backyard, at swirling galaxies and shooting stars. Then the stars dimmed, leaving only moonlight, and the world beyond the tree appeared.

He saw dead grass, the brick wall of the nearby house. There was a hole in the wall, a tiny arm reaching out to him, taunting him, daring him to come closer, to break in to this stranger's home.

Frank approached the wall, and the arm, predictably, retracted. He stood on tip-toes and looked through the opening. The stars were absent here. Frank looked onto an abandoned living room, jagged shadows and shades of plush furnishings.

Frank stepped back from the wall and cursed himself for having left his burglary kit back in Steve's living room. He couldn't go back now for his supplies. He'd risk losing the trail. He would just have to make a tour around the house and hope for an open window.

Frank kept to the shadows, watching for any signs of life in the windows, as he circled the house. His luck was with him, the house remained dark and quiet, and he found a basement window near the back pulled open. There was no screen to worry about, and he was able to slide down through it without much difficulty.

Frank wasn't nervous until his feet settled on the basement carpet of this strange house. If he'd been caught sneaking around in Steve's house, he'd be ostracized, certainly, but not arrested.

Or shot.

But, now that Frank thought of it, Steve did have a cabinet full of guns. He might have gotten shot breaking into Steve's house, too.

Frank wiped his palms on his pants and tried to take deep breaths. His pulse quickened in his ears, making it difficult for him to listen for signs of the house's awakened residents. He took extra care when climbing the basement stairs, placing his weight at the outside of each step. He'd read somewhere that this would help to avoid creaking boards. And it seemed to work, but he found it difficult to hear anything over the beating of his heart. The basement door opened on to a kitchen. Frank saw that the layout to this house was identical to Steve's. Even the appliances and the countertops were the same. Both houses shared the same faulty, flickering bulb over the range.

Frank moved into the living room to find the hole in the wall he'd spotted from outside. He wasn't disappointed. The crack was there. The baby-doll's arm was taunting him. He crept forward and reached his hand out to grab for the silver-gray arm as soon as he was within range. But the arm disappeared a second before he could make his move.

Frank chased after it. He reached his arm into the crack up to his shoulder and flailed around, searching. His arm extended into the endless night of stars that had followed the incubus from tree to tree. He bent his arm at the elbow and felt for the inside of the wall and wasn't able to find it. He brought his right hand toward him far enough that he would be touching his chest had the wall not been in the way, and he didn't see his hand emerge from the wall or feel his palm against his jacket. He pulled his arm from the wall and let his palm rest on the ridge of the crack. He tried to tap his fingers on the inside of the wall, but found that there was nothing there to tap them against. The wall only existed on his side.

Frank took a step back to consider the implications of this and tripped over an object lying in the middle of the floor. His body hit the floor hard, shaking a dozen unseen nick-knacks on the shelves, and the dishes in the kitchen cabinets. Pain shot through his hips. The thing he'd tripped over was wedged in the small of his back. He cursed, reached under his back, and flung the thing across the room. It was a metal cylinder, and it rolled into the big screen television. Frank heard a thud and the twang of a popped spring. And from inside the cylinder, a lamp sprang up from the shadows to a height of seven feet.

Frank cowered, covered his face with his forearms, as the lamp's head exploded into a ball of light. The head bobbled and turned, casting its erratic beam throughout the room. It revealed a mass of intertwined bodies molded together to form the shape of a couch. Frank recognized faces as the swarming spotlight fell upon them. Kristy Kane. Wilma Wonders. Sugar McSweet. All were naked and bound in torturous positions, faces frozen in time, their confused expressions torn between agony and mock lust. The light then scribbled brief glimpses of an overstuffed chair made of more joined bodies. Frank recognized Randy Mayor's tangled chest hair, Ricky Mild's cowboy mustache, Tanya Feast's trademark piercings, and the goldfish tattoo that was the calling card of the one and only Heidi Fleishman Cobb.

Frank crawled across the floor to stop the mad lamp but his left palm knocked against something sharp-edged and wet. It felt like the lid of a soup can. Frank searched the carpet and soon found an empty can. He snatched it up and held it before his face, waited for the spotlight to pass by and illuminate its label.

NoodleZoni, it read.

Then Frank and the word were left in darkness.

When the spotlight returned, the label read, *NoodleZonies*.

Then *CrazyNoodles*.

With each sweep a different brand, *NoodleBites* and *GravyNoodles*.

Chapter 15

Steve retrieved the brown paper bag from the passenger seat. He climbed out of the car and walked briskly up the gravel pathway to Frank's front porch. He hadn't heard from Frank in over a month, nothing until a strange phone call in the middle of the afternoon. Frank had sounded groggy, his speech slurred. He didn't say much, no greeting, no good-bye. "Steve," he'd said, "I need you to bring me over a supply of Serapuems." Steve tried to question him, ask him how he was doing, but the line went dead. And now he was here knocking on Frank's screen door, keeping his mouth tightly closed, careful not to breathe the smell creeping around the cracks in the doorframe. He rattled the aluminum door a few times before deciding to let himself in.

The doorknob had a sticky layer of some unknown substance coating a fine under-layer of crust. He quickly drew back his hand after turning the knob and pushed the door open, wiping his fingers on the peeling wood. He heard a rustling noise as he moved whatever it was that was obstructing the entry. It was like a pile of leaves and branches had drifted up against the door. He poked his head through the crack and found a floor piled almost knee deep with trash. The rustling sound had been a disturbed mound of stale fast food paperboard cartons, crumpled burger sacks, smashed Styrofoam cups, and an assortment of detached plastic no-spill lids with straws still piercing their middles. Steve scanned a carpet of thin microwaveable dinner boxes and used napkins, a hundred restaurant logos smeared and torn and strewn throughout the room. Beer and cola cans popped up everywhere announcing their brands with bold color and brazen design. Cherry Wild. Mega Mountain. Honey Brew. Blue Collar Lager. Plates and bowls teetered in the mess, covered with remnants of unfinished noodles, forgotten sauces, fork-trailed patches of smashed potatoes. Steve spotted an assortment of collapsed water bottles, a casserole dish half full with some ancient meal, an overstuffed grocery bag overflowing with popcorn, two untouched and rotted cantaloupes, piles and piles of laundry, magazines and newspapers, automated-teller receipts and unopened mail, cookie tins, snack chip bags and candy wrappers, tossed onion rings and countless grease-stained French fry sleeves.

"Frank," Steve called out, stepping inside. He kicked a path through the carpet of waste, keeping a close eye on his shoes, being careful not to get anything stuck to them. He raised his voice so that Frank could easily hear him from upstairs. He wanted to give the man a chance to put himself together. He didn't want to repeat his last visit to Frank's house. "Is anyone home?"

Steve looked up when he didn't hear an answer and found Frank sitting on a stool in the middle of the living room, asleep, shirtless, with industrial accordion piping connected to his torso. Three tubes were attached to his back, one between his shoulder blades, one at its base, and one in between. Three more tubes connected to his front, one at the top of his chest, one at his solar plexus, and another just below his navel. The other ends of these tubes were connected to the ceiling overhead. Hastily hammered nails fixed them to cracked and water-stained plaster.

How the piping stayed fixed to Frank's flesh, Steve didn't know.

Frank's eyelids were motionless. He wasn't dreaming.

Steve picked up a collapsed cardboard wine box and used it as a shovel, clearing a path to Frank. When he finally stood over him, he nearly gagged from the smell. And he considered leaving, contacting the county's mental health authority.

"Frank," he said. His voice was quiet. He was afraid that if he opened his mouth too wide that his brother's stench would wash over his taste buds. "Frank, wake up."

Frank snorted and raised his right arm to wipe his nose. He disturbed the tubes, sending waves up to the ceiling. He whimpered and dropped his arm to his side. His chin dropped to his chest, head titled to the right. A brownish line of drool trailed from the corner of his mouth.

Steve considered picking something up from the floor to poke Frank with—less afraid to handle strewn trash than to touch his brother's unwashed skin—but decided that it would be more sanitary to poke his brother's right shoulder on the spot where the most recent nicotine patch was affixed. He pressed the smooth plastic square over and over. He felt like a rude salesman abusing a doorbell.

Frank's eyes opened and registered Steve's presence. They didn't seem surprised. They didn't seem murky either. To Steve's amazement, they were incredibly clear and alert.

"Hey, Steve," Frank said. "Did I leave the front door unlocked again?"

Steve nodded.

"You got the Serapuems."

"What's going on here?"

"You've stumbled upon my investigation."

"I think you're sick, Frank." Steve took a second look at the room, the accordion piping. "You're going to have rats in here."

"I've learned how to study my dreams." Frank scratched his chest hair next to where the top front tube attached. "I can study them while I'm dreaming them."

"What are you talking about?"

"I can tell when I'm dreaming now."

"I hope so."

"You know what I mean. Lucid dreaming. I can examine

them now from a logical perspective. I can even control them sometimes."

"And where has this gotten you, exactly?"

Frank didn't answer.

"You never did go to that interview, did you?"

Frank sniffled again and wiped his nose on his bare forearm.

"You sold your car, didn't you?"

"Who told you that?"

"Jean Daniels from the Old Grocer. She's Jill's cousin."

"People talk."

"You've been riding around on some bike. With a basket on the seat, like some village idiot."

"I'm saving money. I've got groceries to buy."

"You've got a problem."

Frank shook his head, laughed.

"What the hell are these things?" Steve said, disturbing the tubes with a derisive swipe.

"There's nothing wrong with me."

"I bet you haven't been out of the house for at least three weeks. You look like shit."

"I went to the movies last week. I saw this movie about these three kids who live in this post-apocalyptic setting. The whole world is one big third-world country. One night, the kids discover some very strange neighbors up the street. A family with peculiar deformities. To these kids they look like aliens in wheelchairs. Well, the kids find out that their odd neighbors aren't aliens at all. They are the last generation of human beings bred in secret on a space station that had to be grounded right before the world economy went bust. These neighbors look strange because their physiognomy has mutated to adjust to life in space. They are bound to wheelchairs because they can't support themselves in Earth's gravity. It was a pretty good movie, considering that it tried pretty fucking hard to manipulate the old heart-strings."

"What was this movie called, Frank?"

"Suburban Gravity."

"Where is that playing? I've never heard of it."

"Over at Towne Multiplex. I saw a matinee."

"Jill and I were at the Multiplex last week. There's no such movie."

Frank shrugged. "Believe what you want. I'm just telling you."

"What are you doing, Frank?"

"I was getting ready to go to sleep. I just popped the last few Serapuems, getting ready to continue my investigation."

"You're still chasing after that fucking baby-doll arm?"

"It's more than that."

"That's right. You went and named the thing."

"I didn't name it. I found out what it is."

"It's a dream, Frank. Why don't you just let me pay for a few more visits with Dr. Vo? I'm worried that you're going to hurt yourself."

"Dr. Vo can't help me. Besides, I've just about figured it all out on my own now. Vo would have quite a bit of catching up to do."

"What have you figured out?"

"What I have to do."

"What do you have to do?"

"You wouldn't understand."

"You're right. I probably wouldn't."

Frank closed his eyes and nodded his head in agreement. His chin fell to his chest and he began breathing deeply, rhythmically.

"What are you doing, Frank?"

"I'm trying to get some sleep. Give me a call sometime. We'll go play some golf." Frank's mouth turned up in a sarcastic smile. "I promise to take a bath, so you won't be embarrassed."

"Frank," Steve said, "You're lucky— " Then he stopped himself. He saw there was no use continuing. Frank could no longer hear him. He'd already fallen back to sleep.

You're lucky that I don't beat the crap out of you right now, Frank. But I can tell that you just can't help yourself. You just don't know any better.

Steve considered taking the bag of Serapuems with him when he left, but decided to leave them behind. He'd never be able to help Frank if he was pissed at him. He placed the bag gently in Frank's lap, then followed the path he'd cleared through the garbage to the front porch.

Outside.

He locked the door behind him.

Chapter 16

Frank loaded the basket with a duffel bag containing his makeshift burglary kit, kicked his kickstand into the upright position, mounted the bike's plastic seat, and pedaled out into the darkness. He smiled and thought back to the dream in which he'd done the exact same thing, with the same destination in mind, the same intentions. The streetlights cast broad circles over the asphalt; he couldn't ride in the shadows like in his dream. It was cooler tonight and Frank wore gloves and a stocking cap. Steam poured from his nose and mouth. At least two trashcans stood sentry at the end of each driveway; in his dream it hadn't been garbage night. The smell of cheap trash bag plastic was more pungent than that of the rotting meat and vegetables.

Frank heard a dog barking in the distance, then the pattering of paws approaching through autumn leaves. He pedaled faster toward an intersection, but slammed the brakes, squeezed the handle-bars hard, when a shadow leaped into an island of light. The shadow had four legs. It lowered its head and retracted its lips. Its teeth glowed. Steam billowed from its throat.

This can't be a neighborhood dog. It's got the upper body of a wolf.

Frank pushed the bike backwards, slowly, careful not to let the dog out of his sight. He tried to control his pulse, his breathing, tried not to allow his glands to spray the smell of fear. If it had been the middle of the afternoon, he'd just yell at the dog, try to scare it, tell it to get the hell out of the way. But he couldn't do that now, someone would call the police. He went over a map of the neighborhood in his head and considered other routes. But then decided that it probably wouldn't be a good idea to turn his back and run. The dog would almost certainly give chase.

Frank pushed himself a few yards backwards up the hill. He wasn't going to allow himself to be intimidated by this dog. He was going to pedal as fast as he could straight at the beast. Make it get out of his way. He backed up a few more feet, lengthening his runway, and stood up when he pushed down on the pedals. He hunched his shoulders, formed his body into an arrowhead; his arched brow upturned to compete in a feral contest of locked eyes.

Frank moved fast. Cold tears streamed from the corners of his eyes. His heartbeat thrummed in his ears but was soon lost in the beast's deepening growl.

The thing's not moving.

But it was too late to stop. He put his head down and pedaled faster, and prepared for a collision. He closed his eyes and told himself that he was going fast enough now that if it pounced the beast would be deflected off of him and sent sailing into a gathering of trashcans.

But the collision never came, and Frank rode for a long time in darkness.

When Frank realized he'd been pedaling blind for quite some time, he opened his eyes just soon enough to avoid smashing into a cathedral-shaped mailbox.

He took a quick glance behind him. He didn't see the dog, but there was something chasing after him, something much smaller. Frank slowed down in order to focus; a tiny black rabbit was quickly gaining on him. But then Frank realized that the rabbit was not chasing him. It was being chased. The black dog separated itself from the shadows and bounded after it.

Frank pedaled faster. The bike began to tremor and rattled audibly beneath him. He felt the handlebars loosen.

"Shit," Frank said and turned to see the bike's seat teeter off its pedestal and tumble behind him up the street. The rabbit dodged it with two quick, tight turns. But the dog wasn't quick enough. The seat bounced, flipped up from the asphalt, and smacked the animal across the snoot.

Stunned, it stopped to shake off the blow, and then lunged forward with renewed appetite.

Shit.

Frank could barely keep his hands on the handlebars. His sweaty palms were slick against the rubber grips, and the handlebars themselves were becoming looser.

Frank heard deep growling, closer now, and then a snapping sound between his legs. The steering column had come apart. Frank raised his arms and let the handlebars fall away.

Somehow he managed to maintain his balance, and kept pedaling, fear heightening his agility, Frank held his arms out at his sides like a seasoned unicyclist and tried not to think about falling backwards and impaling himself on the exposed end of the seat pedestal. The frame continued to rattle beneath him. He heard screws and bolts falling from their holes, tinkling behind him in the street.

Then the front wheel came off.

Frank was pitched forward. Tucked into a ball, he rolled across hard grit, tearing his clothes, scraping his shoulders, and bloodying his knees. The bike fell to pieces and tumbled after him. When Frank came to a stop, belly-up and exposed, the bike's rear wheel rolled across his gut, and its bare frame smacked painfully across his shins.

Frank didn't stop to collect himself, to think about how badly he might be hurt. He could only think of the shadow chasing him, the shadow's glowing teeth. He pushed himself up, groaning with his injuries, and stood to face his attacker. But he found that he'd managed to gain a good deal of ground as he'd pedaled recklessly onward on his disintegrating bicycle.

Then he saw the black rabbit scurry into an island of light about a hundred yards behind him.

The dog appeared. It leapt down on to its prey, seemingly from high above, as if it had taken to racing across the treetops in its pursuit. The beast trapped the tiny creature and somersaulted with its quarry clamped in its jaws. The dog quickly regained its footing and shook its head back and forth. A froth of spittle sparkled through the streetlights. A much darker spray soon followed, as the beast's teeth let loose the rabbit's blood.

Frank knew this small conquest wouldn't distract the dog for long. It would soon be after him again. He had no choice now but to turn his back and run. His shoulders and knees ached as the rubber soles of his gym shoes pounded pavement. He turned a corner and sprinted three blocks before he had to pause to catch his breath. He bent over, hands on his knees, took deep controlled breaths, and looked down the street behind him. He didn't see the dog. But he knew that it couldn't be far behind. He turned back around and spotted a child's bike parked in a nearby driveway. Its yellow frame shone in the streetlights. Silver handlebar tassels blew in the gentle night breeze. Its metallic-blue banana seat dazzled.

It's a bit small, but it will have to do.

Frank approached the bike, grabbed the handlebars, and jerked the elongated seat beneath him. He noticed a white basket wired to the steering column, and then its strange contents: a pair of sunglasses and a half-closed straight razor. The blade was nicked and stained.

Frank caught movement at the corner of his eye and expected to find the dog crouched next to him, but what he saw was a small white hand.

The hand belonged to a young girl. She held something clutched between her fingers that Frank couldn't identify at first. It resembled a black pompom. But then he followed her hands as she raised it to her head, and watched her tiny fingers as they pulled a wig snugly into place.

Frank wasn't surprised to find that below the false hair

stood a girl who had no face. It wasn't as if a sheet of skin had just grown over her eyes, nose, and mouth, not like a stocking concealing the face of an armed robber. No, there simply were no features. Frank found himself staring at a perfect pink oval.

Frank couldn't believe she was real. He couldn't move, couldn't help but watch the girl reach into the basket and remove the sunglasses. She placed them on her head where her eyes should have been. And Frank couldn't figure out at first how they managed to stay in place, since the girl had no nose, no ears to support them. Then the wind blew back her fake hair to reveal that she'd slipped the arms of her sunglasses through small hoops sewn into either side of her wig.

Her hands returned to the basket and retrieved the straight razor. Her fingers parted the handle from the blade and raised it to her 'face.'

Frank lunged forward to make her stop.

But the girl stepped back and dragged the razor across the bottom half of her blank face, drawing a cartoon frown in her own blood. Then she popped her jaw, stretched it wide, and the frown became a ragged tear, then a gaping red gash.

The girl screamed in agony.

Frank clamped his hands over his ears and took a few steps back, the bike still rolling beneath him. The inside of the girl's mouth was no different than that of a normal child's. His stomach lurched at the innocent pink tongue, the tiny white teeth covered in blood. He gagged, taking his hands from his ears to cover his mouth, and was about to double over and empty his guts, when the screaming stopped.

The night went starkly quiet, suddenly still. Frank managed to take in a breath of cool air, to take control of himself again.

He looked up and found the girl pointing at his face. She

screamed— "Get off my bike!"—lifted the razor over her head and threw it at him. It whizzed past Frank's head and clattered against the windshield of a car parked nearby.

The faceless girl screamed again, raised her hands, curled her fingers into claws.

Frank jumped back, lifted the handlebars of the bike, and accidentally gave the girl an uppercut with its spinning front wheel.

She gave out a short gasp and fell backwards onto the pavement, landing squarely on her bottom, and started to cry.

Her sobs followed Frank as he rode off on her bicycle. He pedaled fast, training wheels clacking. He didn't once consider stopping, though her sobs were not unlike that of any girl who has just been assaulted and had her bike stolen by a strange man.

He wasn't concerned with the faceless girl because the black dog had caught up with him. A deep growl accompanied the sound of shedding tears. Frank heard the dog's breath expelled in heavy bursts, as paws hit the pavement, the beast's lungs and throat setting a dark chugging rhythm.

Frank pushed the little bike as hard as he could, his knees coming up to his chest as he pumped the tiny pedals. He raced down three blocks and turned a corner before the training wheels snapped off and skittered across the asphalt. Less than a block from Steve's house, the handlebars gave way, the seat toppled off, and the front wheel sailed from within its fork and wobbled away.

Frank was determined not to fall this time. As soon as the wheel came loose, he jumped forward and landed on his feet. His heels came down hard, sending sharp pains though his knees and up his spine. But he didn't let the jolting pain stop him. He kept running, heard the bicycle falling to pieces behind him, clattering in the street.

A large part, the frame perhaps, struck the dog.

Frank heard a loud yelp. But he didn't dare look to see how badly the thing might be hurt. The beast's whimpers trailed off as Frank sprinted up Steve's driveway and behind the house to a basement window that he somehow knew would be waiting open.

He dropped to his belly and crawled backwards into the basement, hitting his head on the window frame as he went. He fell as soon as his feet hit the floor, and the basement was filled with stars. He rubbed the base of his skull, it was tender, but there was no blood. When his eyes cleared, and adjusted to the dark, he looked up at the opened window, cursed it under his breath. But he then quickly climbed to his feet and pulled the window toward him, slamming down the latch to seal it shut.

He took a step back to catch his breath, staring at the window as it filled with fog. But it wasn't his breath that clouded the glass. Beyond the pane Frank saw snarling jowls, shining canine teeth.

The dog growled, paced back and forth, and then moved from view.

It's probably gone back for the girl, since it can't get to me.

He sat down in the leather chair in front of Steve's computer desk. He wiped his palms on his jeans, lifted his shirt to dab at his forehead.

He listened.

The house was quiet except for the sound of his own breathing. But then, from outside the basement window, came the sound of rustling leaves. Frank pictured the black dog wrestling in the autumn ground with another rabbit in its jaws, tearing the hide from its bones.

The rustling sound grew louder and Frank dropped his shirt from his eyes to see the window smash to pieces, the black beast sailing though into the basement.

Frank tumbled over the back of the chair and skidded across the coarse all-weather carpet. He pushed himself to his feet.

The beast lunged forward. The top of the chair came down on the backs of Frank's knees and brought him to the carpet again. He heard the leather of the chair snap and puncture in the beast's jaws, and felt the chair lifted off his legs.

He turned and saw the beast jerk its head, whipping the chair out of its way and into a storage closet, derailing a pair of sliding doors.

Frank shot to his feet and climbed the stairs with all four of his limbs. He opened the door leading to the kitchen, sailed through, snapped the lock on the handle, and pressed his back against it. The wood bucked, shook in its frame, as the beast bounded against it.

Frank pressed all of his weight into the door and looked around frantically for something, anything, to put between him and this beast at his back. The flickering bulb above the range poured light into a formal dining room just off the kitchen. And in the dining room, Frank remembered, is where Jill had wanted her piano. Frank had helped Steve move it in. He remembered being grateful then that the thing had wheels, and he was even more grateful now.

He took a chance and left the door unguarded, ran to the old upright piano and pushed, leaning into it, and was overjoyed to find that it rolled smoothly over the stain-resistant carpet. He found it easy to angle the thing into the doorframe leading into the kitchen, and blocked the basement door.

But Frank soon discovered that this barricade did nothing to diminish the beast's efforts. It only grew more determined, throwing itself at the door with more force, sending the door clapping against the back of the piano.

Discordant chords filled the room with each new thrust.

Then the howling started. The dog obviously didn't care for the music it was making. It roared with agony, clawed and scratched, and threw itself at the door.

Frank searched the room for something with which to

defend himself. He saw a wooden block of cutlery on the kitchen countertop. He considered leaping over the piano, but he didn't want to be caught next to the door when the beast burst through. Thankfully, there were two more entranceways that led into the kitchen.

Frank decided to take the long way around and enter through the living room. He ran through jagged shadows, moonlight filtered through the jungle foliage of an adjacent screened-in porch.

Frank slowed down when he saw the pair of erotic drawings, the glare of their glass panes. He stopped when the crack opened in the wall between them.

The silver-gray hand poked out, clumsily rotating, spinning fast, losing its shape like a failed vase relapsing into clay on a potter's wheel. When Frank saw this, he forgot all about knives, though he still distinctly heard the dog's howling at his back. He was suddenly focused again on why he'd decided to come to Steve's house tonight in the first place. When he saw the crack in the wall, the spinning toy arm, his thoughts turned from knives to guns in an instant.

Frank knew where Steve kept his collection. He turned and headed toward the opposite side of the house, toward the garage. But he found his path was blocked.

Jill was standing there, shaking, her arms crossed over her chest. She was wearing a wispy see-through negligée with stockings and garters. Seeing this, Frank expected to find Steve standing close behind her, half-naked and furious. But Jill was alone. Tears ran down her face, glistening in the darkness.

"What the hell's going on here?" She screamed over the howling, the beast knocking against her basement door.

"Where's Steve?"

"Get the hell out!"

"Where's Steve?"

"He's not here. Get out!"

"Where is he?"

"He's in Springfield washing his collectibles."

"What?" Frank said. He ran both hands over the top of his head. "Washing his what?"

"You heard me."

"I need to get one of Steve's guns from the garage."

Jill looked at the knives.

"OK. Never mind. Does Steve have a sledgehammer?" Frank asked, pushing past Jill, making his way toward the garage. "A sledgehammer would be better anyway."

She grabbed hold of his shirt to stop him. "What is going on in the basement? Is there some kind of dog in there?"

"Yes," Frank said. "Let go."

She jerked his arm and his shirtsleeve came off in her hand.

"What do you need a sledgehammer for? Do you plan on killing that dog with it?"

Frank didn't answer. He raced through the house—he could feel Jill following close behind—and threw open the door to the garage. He flipped on the light switch and his eyes fell on a ten-pound sledgehammer. He grabbed its handle with both hands and turned to face Jill.

She flinched.

"Move," Frank said.

Jill quickly stepped aside and let him pass.

Frank raised the hammer over his head, ran the length of the house to the living room, and smashed its head into the wall, opening a second hole. The erotic artwork crashed to the floor. Frank fell back a few steps and took another swing. A third hole appeared and then a fourth and fifth.

Frank pounded the wall as the beast crashed into the basement door behind him. He heaved and smashed. Plaster fell in ragged sheets and crumbled on the carpet. Boards split and cracked, splintered and sprayed with each blow. Frank didn't stop until the hole resembled the proscenium of a small theater.

He dropped the hammer and fell into an easy chair to sweat, chest heaving. His muscles felt as if they'd been pulled from his bones.

The dog had stopped howling. The house was quiet. The door no longer pounded the back of the piano. Frank searched the room. Jill was gone.

She probably ran out into the street when I started tearing down the wall.

Frank turned his attention back to the gaping hole and the darkness beyond. There were no stars, no silvery shapes. The doll's arm was hiding somewhere in the void, afraid to show itself now that Frank could come in after it.

Frank sat and stared at the hole. His fingers combed the soft fabric of the easy chair, and he was thankful not to be sitting on a pile of conjoined porn stars, not to be running his fingers over the hairy forearms of Jerome Kidd or Ricky T-Bone.

He stared at nothing for a long time before the silvery-gray hand re-emerged. It poked out from a spot high overhead, peeking around a place near the top of the hole. Frank tilted his head back into the soft cushion of the chair and watched the toy dance its wobbly dance, but sat up straight when he saw the hand move out of the wall toward him, reaching out as if its forearm were growing at an accelerated pace. It spanned a length of more than eight feet, coming to a stop just a few inches from his nose.

He could now see the tiny silver fingernails of the doll's hand. The creases in its bent fingers were deep. The bolts that joined the hand to the doll's wrist were large and rusted.

Frank looked beyond the hand and saw that the arm hadn't stretched at all. The arm itself was less than six inches in length. It was just stuck to the end of a very long wooden stick.

Frank reached up to touch the hand, and it didn't move. It even allowed him to press his index finger into its palm. Even greeted his touch with a little squeeze.

113

Frank screamed, swiping the thing from his face, knocking it across the room.

The plastic arm flopped against the television, and the tiny hand turned it on. The room was awash in flickering light. The screen filled with the muted image of a talent-show singer, her eyes squinted shut, her arms raised for the end of her ballad.

The doll's arm rose, still held by whatever force lay beyond the wall, and twirled at the center of the screen.

Frank stood, grabbed hold of the stick and tugged it hard toward him.

It didn't move. His hands just slipped down its length.

He took a firmer grip and the stick jerked back, pulling him a foot closer to the hole.

Frank let go, not wanting to be dragged into oblivion. He retreated, and the doll's hand followed, suspended before his face, backing him into the wall opposite the gaping hole.

Then Frank saw the hand wielding the stick emerge from the darkness. Its fingers were wrapped around the handle, forming a fist larger than Frank's head.

The doll's arm smashed through the wall next to his right ear. The stick supporting it snapped to pieces and scattered throughout the room.

The giant fist opened and became a reaching hand, dark gray, almost black. The lines of its palm were deep, shining white in the television's uneven brilliance. Only three fingers and a thumb. The joints shifted against one another as the fingers expanded, as if each segment were covered with cold, chitinous plate armor. The hand looked less like a human hand, and more like a talon belonging to a bird of prey.

The hand shot forward—revealing an arm spotted with rodent hair and the backs of beetles firmly rooted in its flesh. Four giant fingers grabbed the chair Frank had been sitting in just a moment ago and, with one quick jerk, pulled it from the room, out into the darkness.

The hand returned and dragged the couch next, and

then a second easy chair. Soon the room was cleared, except for the television's buzzing, glaring presence.

Then the arm returned to the room, and its great hand spread its fingers across the floor. An elbow emerged, pressing the palm firmly into the carpet. A second arm reached through, another hand took a firm grip.

Then came the monster's head, and the incubus was revealed. Its mouth was wider than Frank was tall. It smiled with pointed teeth, three rows deep, top and bottom. The thing's eyes were two pinched holes, dripping with infection. They dilated, and a pair of black marble eyeballs emerged from beneath the thing's simian brow.

Twin horns sprouted from its massive forehead and scraped against the ceiling. Its mouth opened, groaned in Frank's face, as it dragged the rest of its body into the room.

Frank stood trapped against the wall. He couldn't move. Only a few inches separated him from its flaring nostrils. The thing's body filled the room, crouched down to less than half its height, curled up with its arms wrapped under its bent knees.

Its great mouth moved as if it were trying to speak to him, but didn't make a sound. Its marble eyes retracted into puckered flesh. The floor began to shake.

Frank heard a deep noise, like an airplane taking off, coming from the thing's throat. And then it stood up to its full height, throwing the ceiling and the roof of Steve's house from its back like a magician theatrically throwing off his cape after the final illusion.

Shingles and plaster, beams of wood, fluttered up and disappeared into the night sky, like a thousand birds taking flight.

Frank craned his neck and saw stars, the night sky, just beyond a pair of glistening horns.

The thing looked down at Frank. He couldn't see its eyes, its teeth. Its features were now lost in shadow. But he knew that he was being watched. The thing's gaze kept him still. He couldn't turn his eyes from the twisted horns. The creature's shoulders shook as if it were quietly laughing.

A crop of tentacles grew from the back of its neck. Six fleshy strands stretched and lengthened, whipped around the horns, snapped in a mindless frenzy.

Then suddenly the tentacles dropped and hung writhing on either side of the thing's torso. They continued to grow until they reached the plush carpet at Frank's feet.

Frank turned to run, but his time to escape had passed. He now understood the black dog and the faceless girl. They had known where he was headed—and what he'd planned to do. They'd been placed in his path to stop him, to scare him awake before it was too late.

And now the tentacles were on him. The three tentacles branching from the left of the thing's neck were firmly rooted to Frank's back. A second later, his belly and chest were connected to the three strands of flesh trailing up the beast's right side. The tentacles had no trouble finding and penetrating his six dead spots. They pricked his skin like clusters of intravenous needles, pumping him with a stinging coldness.

Frank closed his eyes in surrender, let the incubus overtake him, let it fill him with its heavy fluids. He felt a strange wet warmth press against the inside of his face, slithering lumps moving under the skin of his chest. The flesh of his thighs wriggled in fattened waves.

The numbness of his six dead spots expanded to cover his entire body. He felt nothing. No pain.

Frank blinked, opened his eyes, the incubus still loomed, and he found that he was no longer frightened.

The night sky was just beginning to fade into a morning mist when the incubus came apart. Its hair fell and its skin sloughed from its arms. Its horns broke free from its skull and slammed to the floor a few feet from where Frank stood.

But he didn't flinch.

A hail of giant jagged teeth fell and lodged themselves deep into the floorboards.

The demon's skin gathered in a puddle at Frank's feet. Its muscles liquefied. Its black bones rocked and creaked. The bars of its ribcage looked like a prison built for a baby dragon, but crumbled to dust in a faint wind, and were swallowed in a sea of melted flesh.

The demon's naked spine tottered like a kindling tower built by an idiot child. Its skull rolled forward and splashed down and disappeared in a puddle of its own flesh, like it had fallen into deep waters.

The incubus was gone. Its remains swirled at Frank's feet.

He was alone with the television, with an extreme close-up of a severe woman selling pain relief. The tentacles were still implanted deep in his flesh; the opposite ends now moving through the muck.

Searching.

But then, when the liquid waste that was once the incubus began to recede, Frank realized that the tentacles weren't looking for something. They were thirsty. They were siphoning the thing's remains, drinking them, sucking the liquid incubus into Frank's torso, filling him up.

The tentacles overtook Frank's body, dragged him throughout the room as they vacuumed the remains puddled in the carpet.

When the floor was dry and clean, the tentacles retracted and disappeared inside of Frank, leaving no trace on his flesh.

Frank touched a spot just below his sternum. It was no longer dead.

Chapter 17

Frank opened his eyes and was glad to see that Steve had gone. He was overjoyed to actually feel the painful tug of the adhesive he'd used to secure the six accordion tubes to his skin. He grabbed the tube fixed at the center of his chest with both hands and yanked it free. He screamed, and laughed with relief. He smiled down at the circle of raised blood on his sternum, and shuddered. He stood and ripped the remaining tubes from his body with five curt yelps. And he stood there, breathing heavily, smiling, eyes welling with tears, and reveled in the sensation of blood running over flesh once lost to him.

Frank turned, stamped across a carpet of EZ-Meal boxes and Taco House bags to the front window and searched the driveway and the street for Steve's car. He was certainly gone. And he'd been a good brother and left the pills behind. But Frank looked at the crumpled DrugMart logo and knew that he would never open the bag. He didn't need Serapuems anymore. Tonight would be the end of it.

Frank reached down the front of his stained jeans and made his daily collection. His hand returned with a harvest of his own filth slathered across his fingers. He rubbed his fingertips together and rolled his waste into a ball about the size of a schoolyard marble. He rolled the 'marble' gently across the blood pooled on his chest, rolled it between his palms, and then held it admiringly before a squinted eye.

This is it. The last bit.

Frank's feet crunched sardine tins and processed cheese wrappers as he rushed from the living room, over broken pizza box cardboard and the wax sleeves from frozen beef pies as he slogged through the kitchen to his basement door. He kept it locked and the key close to him at all times, in the right front pocket of the pants he'd been wearing for three months straight. He unlocked the door and took the first few steps down, closing the door gently behind him.

He walked to a mini-fridge near his washer and dryer and opened the door. On top of a cache of assorted beer cans lay a cookie tin with a green linen napkin draped over it. Frank removed the tray and rested it on top of the refrigerator. He peeled the napkin back and revealed his creation, the tiny figure he'd been molding for months. Although the smell that wafted up at him was horrible and overwhelming, his tearing eyes still traveled the tiny body with pride, the miniature man sculpted from his own bodily waste. It was only a few inches long, no bigger than a boy's collectible action figure. It lay on its back as if awaiting a medical operation. Its torso, head, and limbs were formed from a compound of dried skin, eye paste, mucus, and semen. The features of its face were drawn with nail clippings. The hair that covered its head and body was pulled from Frank's arms. The curlies between its legs once belonged to Frank.

Frank rolled his new ball of 'clay' between his fingers, concentrating, planning, rolled it between his palms. He then carefully sculpted the lump, accenting and smoothing with a paperclip and a pen cap. Twenty minutes later, he held a tiny penis and scrotum. He placed this finishing touch between the figure's legs and carefully blended it in with the lines of its body, rearranging the pubic hair around its center piece.

Satisfied, he moved the tray from the fridge top and carried it over to a dark corner of the basement. He placed it on a wooden block he'd spray-painted black, next to a dusty square car battery and a converter with metal coils branching from its top. Frank pulled the string hanging overhead and a bare bulb shook to life, unsteady and dim. He turned his tiny man carefully on to its side and then began to sort through the wire coils. He unwound one, straightened it, and then bent it down to touch the sculpture at the top of its chest. Frank pushed and the wire pierced through and shivered, set firmly in place. He then straightened another wire and plugged it into the little man's solar plexus, and another just below its navel. Frank attached the remaining three wires to the figure's back, one between the shoulder blades, one at its base, and another in between. He made sure that all six connections were firmly set and then flipped the switch on the converter to bring the thing to life.

Rancid smoke began to rise immediately from the cookie tray. Frank stepped back and coughed, his eyes watering. He doubled over and gagged, fell to his knees, and his chest heaved. Vomit burned the back of his throat and then splashed onto the cement floor between his hands, spraying his wrists and forearms. Frank's eyes were closed, and he listened to his heavy breathing and the sizzling noise coming from the metal tray, his baking filth. He tasted the miracle of new life springing forth from decay.

He forced his eyes open, wanting to bear witness, and thought he saw, through smoke and tears, a shape rise from the tray. He was almost certain that the tiny man was moving, struggling to its feet, standing to meet the world. Smoke rose around it as if it were a god of lava rising from the mouth of a volcano.

Frank tried to greet this new life but his throat was raw, clogged with snot and vomit. And he heard footsteps, several pairs of shoes stomping down his basement stairs. Deep, official voices. A man retching.

"What the hell is that smell?"

"He's started a fire." His brother Steve's muffled voice.

"What is he burning? Shit?"

Frank cleared his eyes and saw the man who asked this question. He was a police officer. His uniform was bulky, a deep blue, almost black in the basement's spare lighting. A second officer came into view and his eyes widened as he looked past Frank at the smoke rising from the tray.

He's amazed to see the miracle I've worked. He's awed by the new life I've brought into the world.

Frank turned his face to the intruders. It shone with a fierce pride, which soon turned to rage when the officers ran past him, pushing him out of the way, to stomp the fire out. Their black boots crumpled the tray and smeared the tiny figure to an ashy sludge before Frank could stop them.

But he attacked anyway. He needed to avenge the death of his creation. He lunged forward at the pair of officers, hands raised, fingers curled, ready to rip their eyes from their sockets, intent on smashing their noses into their faces. But he never made contact. Both officers were young and well-trained. They raised their batons and together knocked Frank unconscious with two sharp raps to his skull.

Chapter 18

Steve walked into the smoky waiting room of the Greater Springdale Center for Psychiatric Health and saw his brother sitting by a window, arm draped over the ledge, staring out at a parking lot lined with trees and peaceful landscaping, muted colors, chosen carefully so as not to excite the patients. Steve had only seen Frank once before in the year since he'd been committed. The doctors had felt that isolation was the best thing for Frank, quiet and order. They feared any news from outside might send him spiraling back to the place from which he'd fought so hard to return. Frank was dressed in a gray sweater Jill had sent him for his birthday and the green slacks Steve had sent him for Christmas. He looked incredibly thin. The meds appeared to have taken his appetite and all the color from his face. Frank turned and Steve saw creases at the corners of his mouth and eyes that shouldn't have been there for at least ten more years.

"It's good to see you, Frank."

Frank stood and reached out his hand. Steve grabbed it and dragged Frank into him and hugged him.

"So what's going on?" Frank asked, his voice muffled in Steve's shoulder. "Are you my guardian now?"

Steve laughed. "No. I'm not my brother's keeper." He patted Frank on the back. "I'm just picking you up. You're free to go."

"They can't keep me any longer."

"No. They can't keep you."

Steve stretched out his arms, holding Frank's shoulders,

and smiled. His smile wasn't returned.

Frank was still on heavy medication. His eyes were listless. He turned his head away and his attention returned to the window. His eyes followed a station wagon moving slowly through the parking lot. "You're taking me home."

"That's right."

"I don't think Jill would like that very much."

"She wouldn't like it at all. I'm not taking you to my house. I'm taking you to yours."

"Oh," Frank said, turning away, freeing himself from his brother's embrace. "I just assumed that the bank had taken it back."

"No," Steve said. "I've made some arrangements."

Frank picked up a newspaper off the windowsill, folded it in thirds, turned his back to Steve, and walked to the door. "I'll pay you back," he said. "It will take a while. But I'll pay you back."

"Don't worry about it."

"I want to."

"Then don't worry about it for a while. All right?" Steve caught up with Frank, pushed the door open for him, and followed him out into green hallways filled with milling men in paper-thin gowns, sleepy eyes and stuttering lips.

Steve squeezed his brother's shoulder. "All right?"

"All right. I appreciate it."

"No, you don't," Steve said, and instantly wished he hadn't. The last thing he wanted to do was initiate an argument.

"It's called absence of affect," Frank said. "It comes with swallowing a handful of psychotropic drugs with every meal."

"I'm sorry, Frank."

"Don't be. I'm too tired."

· · · · · ·

Frank and Steve sat in Frank's driveway in uncomfortable silence for a long time before Steve reached over and opened the glove compartment for Frank's keys. Three keys dangled on a simple silver ring: front door, back door, and garage. He shook them and dropped them into Frank's palm.

"Thanks." Frank shoved open the passenger door and stuck his foot out. "Sorry if I don't sound like I mean it."

"Get some sleep." Steve put the car into gear and pressed a button on his armrest, rolling up Frank's window. "I'll call you in a few days."

Frank groaned as he pulled himself up and out of Steve's car. His ankles seemed weak as he traversed his gravel walkway. He climbed the steps to the porch and pulled open the screen door. He stood there with his keys and watched his brother drive off. Steve waved.

Frank didn't wave back. He turned the key in his front door and stepped inside his home for the first time in over a year. The living room was empty. The walls were clean of pictures and cracks. The house smelled musty, closed up. The smell of household cleaner still lingered in the air.

Frank walked into the kitchen and placed the wrinkled bag containing his prescriptions on the counter next to a line-up of spray bottles standing proud. Like show horses. Windows Plus X. Surface Shine. OMOX. Toilet Cop.

The dishes on the drying rack were covered in a layer of dust. But the place was clean.

Frank rinsed a glass and drank, gulped, and dribbled water down his shirt.

His medication.

He'd been written a prescription for endless thirst. He took two pills and drank two full glasses of water, rinsed the glass, and returned it to the drying rack.

· · · · · ·

Frank's bedroom was empty, save for a single twin bed and a small oak dresser. They looked new. All of his old furniture had been removed from the house. The carpet had been stripped from the floors and the exposed wood was buckled in places and deeply scarred. The walls were stark white.

Twilight had long ago disappeared and the windows now looked on a reflection of Frank's bedroom. The light fixture over his bed blared with three bare bulbs. There were no blinds or curtains on the windows, so he quickly flipped down the light switch.

He didn't like what he saw reflected in the window.

Frank hadn't seen his own reflection since the morning he woke up in the Greater Springdale Center for Psychiatric Health.

He undressed in darkness, draped his clothes over the top of the dresser, and slipped into a tightly made bed that had never been slept in. The air was dry beneath the covers. Dry and warm.

Chapter 19

Frank woke up in his twin bed, opened his eyes, and surveyed his bedroom. He hadn't changed a thing since being released. He hadn't hung a picture or added a single piece of furniture in seven months. The only item that wasn't in the room when he'd moved back in was a golf bag propped up in the corner. Only three clubs poked out of the top, a putter, a driver, and a wood. His brother had given them to him as a present over three months ago and today was the first day he'd agreed to a game. The season was almost over. It was cold and Frank didn't want to get out of bed.

But he did. He sat up and rubbed his face, groaned as he stood, and grunted as he slowly made the bed.

He unlocked his bedroom door and went through the short hallway and into the bathroom and showered. He toweled off and brushed his teeth with the medicine cabinet open, mirror facing the wall.

He hesitated and scowled at every piece of his clown suit as he put them on. He wore loud argyle pants, a yellow shirt, and a checkered duffer's cap. He carried his clubs downstairs and set them down next to a shoe box by the front door. His living room was still barren.

His footsteps echoed as he walked into the kitchen. The refrigerator hummed. The counter tops were bright in the early morning sun. The glasses in the drying rack sparkled. He unfastened the wire tie from a loaf of rye bread and set it gently on the counter, taking special note of exactly where he placed it. He buttered his bread, slid it onto the rack in the toaster oven, and closed the door. He drank a glass of orange juice and two glasses of water while he waited. He took the loaf of bread and spun it closed, twisting it shut again, and retied it.

The oven's lever popped.

Frank crunched his toast and washed it down with two more glasses of orange juice.

He washed his hands and then the glass and returned it to the rack. He dried his hands and walked to his front door. He shouldered his clubs, tucked the shoe box under his arm, and stepped out into the light.

Frank locked the door behind him, set his clubs aside, and sat on a simple wooden bench. He removed the lid from the shoe box, pulled his socks up, and slipped on a pair of white golf shoes.

Steve's car pulled into the driveway. Frank's cleats scraped across the cement porch and crunched on his gravel walkway.

He saw Steve waving at him through his windshield and pretended like he didn't notice. The trunk popped open as Frank approached. He walked around to the back of the car and tossed his clubs on top of two golf bags overflowing with gear. Both belonged to Steve. Frank closed the trunk and walked around to the passenger door. The window rolled down and Steve said, "Good morning."

Frank opened the door and plopped down into the bucket seat next to Steve. He raided the glove compartment, grabbed a pack of mints he knew would be there, and popped one in his mouth.

"Mint Chews?" Frank asked. "Why'd you switch brands?"

Steve reached over and slapped the glove compartment shut. "They stopped making MiNiMiNts about two or three months ago. I lived for a while on stockpiles."

"They're not bad." Frank chewed. "But no MiNiMiNts."

"You're right about that."

Not much else was said for the remainder of the drive to Steve's country club. Frank hadn't found the need to talk much since he'd been released. It seemed that he was expected not to say much.

But Frank didn't keep quiet because he didn't have anything to say. He had something that he truly wished he could say to his brother, but knew that he never would. He wished he could tell him that he'd stopped seeing his own reflection the morning after he woke up in the institution. He'd never even told the doctors about that. He'd wanted to leave the place one day. He knew that telling people you can no longer see your reflection sounds crazy. But it was true. He hadn't seen his own face in nearly two years.

He wasn't like a vampire. Frank did cast a reflection. He did see a face reflected in the mirror—just not his face.

· · · · · ·

The golf cart hummed and jostled and landed Steve and Frank at the eleventh tee. Steve was on his third beer and Frank had played so poorly so far that he'd stopped keeping score on the fifth hole. Steve stumbled out of the cart, crushed his beer can and stuffed it in a plastic grocery bag he'd been using for empties. He belched and shook out his arms, chose his club, and stepped up to the tee. He squinted down the fairway, shifted his grip on the earth, and swung beautifully. The ball arced high and sailed straight, landing on the green with three gleeful bounces.

Steve turned back to Frank, smiling, obviously searching for a compliment.

"Nice one," Frank said, his back turned, climbing out of the cart. He lugged his bag over to the tee. "It's too bad you're playing against yourself."

Steve laughed. "That's kind of the point in golf."

Frank shrugged his bag off his shoulder and onto the ground. It clanked loudly as it fell to the grass. He unsheathed his wood, planted the little white ball at his feet, and swung without even taking a single glance down the fairway. The ball flew up, almost perfectly vertical, and Steve and Frank took a step back to avoid it coming down on their heads.

"Whoa," Steve said as he watched the ball land next to a monster divot Frank had unearthed with his swing.

Frank held the head of his club before his face to inspect it, as if blaming it for his bad swing, and saw a dripping orifice reflected in its metal label. The hole puckered and an eye spat forth. It stared back at him, gleaming like a black pearl. Frank turned the club so that its label no longer faced him and slammed it down hard against the ground. And, shaking with rage, he took another swing.

More dirt flew to the wind.

Steve laughed again. "You forgot the ball, Frank. It's easier to hit if you have it in front of you."

Frank pounded the dirt until his club snapped.

"Frank." Steve cracked open another beer. "Take it easy. I was just kidding."

Frank ignored his brother and reached down for his bag.

"Hey," Steve said, and took a serious swallow of beer, "don't make me stand here and watch you smash all your clubs. We'll just go home."

Frank plucked his driver and his putter from his bag and tossed them into the grass. He reached his arm deep inside and removed a bundle wrapped in a grease-stained rag.

Frank looked up at his brother and, with tears welling in his eyes, said, "Better run," and then unwrapped the AG-9 submachine gun.

"Is that my gun?" Steve asked.

"Yeah."

"How'd you get that?"

"While you were sleeping. Like I said, better run."

Steve didn't say anything else. He didn't ask Frank what he was doing. He didn't try to talk him out of doing something stupid. Steve looked at the gun and ran. Fast. He was over a hill and beyond a row of trees before Frank could find a magazine and load his weapon.

Frank took aim first at the golf cart. He held the AG-9 with both hands and squeezed the trigger. The plastic cart puckered and spat, smoked and sparked. It shuddered and rolled backwards as if it were consciously trying to escape. Frank emptied his magazine into the thing, reloaded, and continued to shoot at the cart until it was just scraps of torn fiber glass and no longer fun to shoot at.

Frank turned the flashing barrel to the fairway and sprayed the ground. The hammer-like bang of his weapon muffled his senses, blocked out all other sounds. Its vibrations dominated. It became all that he felt. A deep sense of satisfaction overcame him as he watched clumps of turf jumping to the air in scores.

Frank stopped firing to catch his breath and heard the screams of approaching sirens.

Frank had a vision of the future. He saw the police arrive. He saw himself firing his gun over their heads to provoke them. He heard their return fire. He looked down and saw three tiny gunshot wounds perfectly spaced down the center of his torso, and, as if he were standing outside himself, the much larger exit wounds down his spine.

He smiled, nodded his approval, and opened fire on the fairway again. The police would be there soon, and they would do exactly what he wanted them to do. They would put holes in him, unleashing the demon nested in his flesh.

About the Author

Gregor Xane lives and writes in Ohio.

Connect with him online:

blog: gregorxane.blogspot.com

twitter: @GregorXane

goodreads: goodreads.com/GregorXane

e-mail: gregorxane@gmail.com